I0619839

Revenge

Princes of Powell – Book 1

By Carmen Black

Published by Scarlet Lantern Publishing

Copyright © 2020 by
Carmen Black & Scarlet Lantern Publishing

All rights reserved.

This is a work of fiction. Names, characters, businesses, places, events and incidents are either the products of the author's imagination or used in a fictitious manner. Any resemblance to actual persons, living or dead, or actual events is purely coincidental.

This book contains sexually explicit scenes and adult language.

Prologue

I muscled in a deep breath before striding across the lawn toward the cluster of trees that took up the front of Woodman High's sand-colored building. I spotted Pierre leaning against one of the trees, just like always.

He nodded at me. "Hey, Kat."

Since he was a few inches shorter than me, and I've taken every opportunity to ruffle his mop of dark hair, I didn't hold back now.

"You find your phone yet?" he asked.

"Of course not."

I'd gotten home from school about a week ago to find that my phone wasn't in my pocket, backpack, or anywhere it should've been. Checking all six of the classrooms in my schedule and the school's lost and found had turned up nothing.

Pierre leaned back against the tree. This was the last time I would see him like this—leather messenger bag, white button-down, neon headphones hugging his neck. Sweetheart, schoolboy who wouldn't hurt a fly. We've been friends since day one of Woodman High, and I'd never let him go, not for the world.

Sucked that we were both off to better days ahead.

Pierre looked around at the thin crowd of students clustering around the entrance, those who had spotty attendance records or a genuine affinity for stuffy cinderblock rooms. Then he looked back at me. "We're losers, aren't we?"

I smirked. "Completely."

If it weren't for Pierre's acceptance to a university halfway across the world, then I wouldn't have shown up today. This was my one chance to say goodbye.

The bell rang and we started toward the entrance of the building.

"You know what?" Pierre said. "This day is blessed."

"How so?"

He reached an arm around my shoulders, pulling me into a loose headlock as we pushed through the wide red doors.

"Think about it. The few fuckers who have wreaked hell on our lives these past four years won't be here. We're free. For one day, we're—"

I stopped short, breaking away from Pierre's hold.

"Fuck," he muttered. " I spoke too soon."

Sprawled across the floor of the lobby were Elliot, Felix, and Leo—the school princes. Calling them gods wouldn't even be a stretch. They made both girls and school administrators fall to their knees at the snap of their fingers, at one word, at one gesture. They made this world spin in any direction they pleased.

"Why are they here?" Pierre hissed. "Aren't they too good for the last day of school?"

I looked at Elliot, at his short, jet-black curls and his black dragon tattoo. I'd never seen it before. I traced the tattoo with my eyes as it snaked over his shoulder and around his collarbone to end with the serpent licking at his ear.

The three of them had set up bright-colored beach chairs, reclined to their lowest setting, in the center of the lobby. Elliot straddled the middle chair, while Felix stretched out to his right and Leo to his left. All three wore pairs of pink cat eye sunglasses and tight speedo swim trunks.

Nothing else.

Elliot removed his sunglasses and stared right at me.

He was tall—they were *all* tall—with eyes like a tiger's, changing from amber to green depending on the light. His skin was pale enough to be cause for mockery, but he made it edgy with the dark contouring of his tattoo.

"Hey!" He flashed a bright white smile. "I have something for you."

"Ignore him," Pierre muttered, grabbing my arm to pull me past the group. "Let's go."

Before we could escape the spotlight, he leapt up from his chair and pulled something out of the tote bag that was leaning against his chair. He spun around, holding out the object toward me.

My cellphone.

Fury boiled in my gut.

As other students began to enter, they laughed, whipping out their phones to snap photos of the school's newest spectacle. Class clowns gain popularity if they're classy, but these bad boys were beyond clowns. They won over the majority of the school with their old money, lethal good looks and legendary pranks, but their charm was only cosmetic.

Thanks to him and his ass-hat friends, I've stepped into Woodman every day for the past four years feeling like fresh meat. So much for the title of second-semester senior.

"Give it back to her, Elliot," Pierre tried, but his words might as well have come out as a hoarse whisper. I couldn't blame him. He'd never been able to stand up to Elliot. In the grand scheme of things, I'd consider this his most gallant attempt.

"Holy shit," I heard someone say. I turned around to find the crowd of students staring into their phones, snickering. They kept glancing up between me and Elliot.

"Oh, damn," a boy said.

"Slut alert," a girl giggled, standing beside him.

They kept going. The voices blended together, throbbing in my head. Sweat beaded on my temples. They weren't taking photos of Elliot and his friends. They were looking into the phone screens, *reading* something.

I turned to look back at Elliot, only to find myself face-to-face with the screen of my phone, which Elliot had shoved into my face. He had up my Instagram page, and a photo under my account, with thousands of likes—way more than I'd ever been capable of garnering in a little over a week.

It was a screenshot of some notes in my phone. Notes I'd written about him.

About how *fucking* much I liked him.

"That's *so* embarrassing."

"Oh my God."

"This is, like, psycho."

"Ell, you better run, man."

The voices wouldn't stop. More students jammed into the lobby.

Pierre reached for my arm again to drag me away, but I lashed out for my phone—and instead of missing Elliot's wrist, I smacked right into him. He stumbled to the floor, phone still tight in his grasp, while I rolled off his chest to the floor. My cheeks burned.

Of course, the one day he isn't wearing shirt is the day I impale his abs with my dirt-packed fingernails.

"Hey!" A school security guard burst onto the scene just as I lifted myself off the ground. "What's going on here?"

Elliot was already bounding down the hall. Before whipping around the corner, he paused to taunt me by flashing that bright smile, waving my phone above his head.

"Kat," Pierre called, "don't."

Ignoring him, I tore down the hall. I didn't give a shit about Elliot showing the world what basically qualified as pornographic love letters penned for no one's eyes but my own. It was the last day of school. I didn't care what these bystanders thought of me, and didn't care that he hated me—but if I was leaving Woodman forever, I wanted to leave with a grand fucking flourish.

He pushed through the door into a stairwell and I slammed my shoulder against it as the metal came swinging back to hit me.

"You know how to hunt," he shouted as he stumbled down onto the last landing. My phone flew out of his hands and smashed against the brick wall in front of him. He turned around and backed himself against the wall, raising his arms behind his neck. "Feral Kat."

I paused at the top of the set of steps.

"If you're gonna pounce, do it," Elliot said, and spat onto the floor. "Come at me."

I continued down the steps, my heart pounding so hard that I could feel the blood swelling up in my face. One more step and I was at Elliot's eye level.

"I'm curious," he said, eyes dropping to my chest, "where *do* you get the inspiration for your stories? 'Cause I'm not seeing much action, sweetheart."

I snapped.

"Just because I'm a virgin doesn't mean I intend on staying one," I blurted, and bit my tongue.

"Yeah," he snorted, lowering his voice as I came closer. "I could tell."

A hundred thundering heartbeats later, we stood inches apart. Elliot raised his eyebrows, stretching out against the wall even more. He *knew* he was godly, that his body mirrored Michelangelo's David, the Discobolus of Myron, fucking King Odysseus himself, every Greek ideal of the highest sensual order.

I smiled sweetly at him. Then my hand darted out, grabbing his cock through the material of his Speedo. Digging my nails into his bulk, I yanked him forward.

"What the fuck?" Elliot hissed.

He crashed against me, and I kept him there for a moment before shoving him back, pinning him against the wall.

"Well?" he said, burning holes deep into my eyes. "Go ahead."

I wanted to.

I wanted to grab him by the neck and sink my teeth into the scales of his dragon tattoo, claw my fingers through his storm of curls, hold his hand in mine and shove it up my own skirt.

But most of all, I wanted to beat his fucking brains out.

Instead, I let go of his shoulders. Without breaking my eyes from his gaze, I pulled on the elastic waistband of his trunks, and dipped my other hand past the thin fabric until the tips of my fingers brushed against his cock.

He let out a heavy breath. I wrapped my hand around his shaft—it was thick, full, heat coursing like lightening through his skin. I started pumping, my hand trembling as it slid up and down his shaft. Heat rushed down my belly.

This couldn't have been real.

"Fuck," he breathed, his hands ghosting up my arms. "What… are you…"

If he wanted me to stop, he could've stopped me. He had the advantage of being a foot taller than me and having muscles that could match David Beckham's come next semester in college. He could've pushed me to the ground, slapped me, pulverized me with one glance. But he did nothing.

Just as well.

I wasn't here to backtalk him or explain myself.

Suddenly, I stopped handling him as he gasped, his nails slicing into my shoulders. I waited for him to look up at me, and as soon as we made eye contact, dragged my nails along the length of his shaft. Liquid heat surged between my fingers.

Panting, he dropped his hands from my shoulders, collapsing against the wall. I slipped my hand out of his trunks, and he flinched as I snapped the elastic band back against his waist.

Revenge felt so sweet.

"Thanks for an unforgettable four years," I whispered, leaning into his ear. "Asshole."

1

Welcome to my new life in three, two…

One.

I let out the breath I was holding as I pushed open the door of my dorm room to a girl with crimped blonde hair, pink lipstick and an off-shoulder crop top. Her hand rested on the inside door handle.

"You must be Kathleen," she said, smiling as she looked me up and down—at my purple-dyed hair, oversized hoodie and fishnet stockings. Then frowned.

"Yeah," I replied, replicating her grin. "And you're—"

"Vivian," she replied, sticking on that hot pink smile again. "My friends call me Vivi."

I smiled back. "My friends call me Kat."

Vivian stepped back from the door, allowing me to step into the room. "Well, we're roomies now, so all labels are blurred now, anyway."

"Ha," I laughed weakly, raising my eyebrows as I dragged my duffel bag into the cramped space. Based on the tone of her voice, I certain that how we'd label one another in the coming weeks would be anything but 'friends'. At the end of the day, we'd just have to put up with one another. That was that.

I took in a breath.

No. This was my time to start over. I had to *try*.

"So," I began, hefting my duffel up onto the naked mattress. At least she'd left me window side. "How was the trip over here? Did you move in today?"

According to the sparse three-sentence-long email the university had sent out to me a week ago, all I knew about my roommate was her last name, and the fact that she was from California. But hey, conversations have to start somewhere.

"I actually moved in a couple days ago," she said, as if a couple days was two years, nodding to the explosion of cosmetics on the vanity, and her bed, which was made up with layers of throw pillows, bras and hangers packed with miniskirts and tube tops. "Is that all you brought?"

I didn't understand until I saw her eyes move to my bag.

"Oh," I laughed. "My mom's gonna send some boxes up. These are just clothes to get me by for now."

I looked back at the pile of outfits on her bed and noticed that her closet was stuffed enough to warrant it hanging open a crack. A scattered trail of heels drew the boundary between her side of the room and mine, which was soulless as a prison cell between the metal desk and chair, skeletal bed frame, and nothing else.

Her side, on the other hand, was as lived in as a teenage girl's room could be in eighteen years of growing up, meaning, messy as hell—an incredible feat considering it'd been two days. Though tidiness was usually the last thing on my radar, even I couldn't trash a room as quickly as she had.

"Well, as long as it isn't anything similar to what you're wearing now, then yeah," she said, shrugging, "you should get by."

I pressed my lips into a flat line meant to emulate a grin.

"There's a meet-and-greet type thing," she continued, grabbing her purse from the hook beside her vanity. "You should come."

The pit that had started forming in my gut flipped into butterflies, and I lifted my head a little higher. "Why not?"

She felt awkward. That had to be it. I wasn't expecting to come into my first year of college making friends left and right, especially not after getting used to being Elliot's punching bag for four years in a row. But I was past that. Maybe we didn't click right off the bat, but she'd invited me to join her. At least she was trying.

I couldn't give up on my social life now.

She opened the door without saying anything more and I followed her into the hall. Our neighbors were blasting hip-hop, and the bass drowned out the voices within. A girl stood in the doorframe of the following room, taping faux flowers and leaves to the front of the door. We made eye contact.

"Looks good," I said, slowing my pace long enough to butter her up a bit more. "Gardenias, right?"

Her brown eyes lit up. "Yeah," she answered, tilting her head as if to get a better look at me. "How did you—"

"I like Billie Holiday," I said, grinning at her reaction, and decided to throw in a shrug for a show of modesty. "She was famous for putting gardenias in her hair."

"Ugh, I *love* Billie," she gushed, her smile spreading even further. "What's your name by the way?"

"Kathl*ee*-een," Vivian called. We both turned our heads to look at her. She was standing at the end of the hall, twirling the lanyard for the room key around her index finger. "Stop admiring the marijuana leaves or we'll be late."

I let out a flimsy laugh and started to back away. The girl smiled in sympathy.

"I'm Tara," she said. "See you around, Kathleen?"

"Kat," I replied, "and definitely."

I found myself smiling a genuine smile for the first time since I'd arrived at Freeman. See, Kat? New people, fresh start. I was expecting worse, to be honest. I was on someone's good side. Pierre would be so proud.

Vivian whipped around the corner of the hall as soon as I caught up with her.

"I knew her in high school," she called over her shoulder, without consideration for the fact that we were less than three yards away from the girl's room. "Total pothead. Ask her for a cheap deal if that's what you're looking for. Heard she's already growing weed under her bed."

"Bet you've heard a lot of things," I muttered under my breath. Vivian must have heard it, because she threw me a close-lipped smile so flat she could've shattered her teeth.

I was familiar with girls like her back at Woodman. They're simple—they like those who are like them, and they don't like those who aren't. The best part? They have zero qualms about letting everyone in on their social preferences.

We reached the elevator without getting into a cat fight, so for that, I gave myself another mental pat on the back. She jabbed the button with a French-manicured fingernail. We were on the fifth floor. My worst fear was upon us—if the elevator system was crappy, I'd have to stare at her, waiting in an awkward silence that'd last way too long for my liking. Crossing my arms, I settled against the wall opposite from where she stood scrolling through her phone. Maybe now was the time to start some more small talk.

"Hey," someone said, just as I opened my mouth. A boy approached us from the other end of the floor. "You guys know where the Arena is?"

Vivian looked up from her phone. As he joined us near the elevators, the boy looked between the two of us, but his gaze landed on Vivian. No doubt, it'd stay there the rest of the way. He was just like her. Tall, blonde, varsity jacket. In other words, alpha male to her alpha female.

"Yeah," Vivian replied, then rolled her eyes. "We're going to try to make some new enemies at that mixer thing."

"Great minds think alike," he said, flicking his green eyes to me. "You guys roommates? Old friends?"

Vivian let out a snort. "The former."

I returned her line of a grin and dug my phone out from my purse. Since it was apparent that I was about to be a third wheel to their exclusive acquaintanceship, might as well use the time to distract Pierre.

"Where you from?" the boy asked.

"Sacramento. You?"

"Santa Barbara."

"No kidding!"

"Nice to meet another West Coaster out here. There aren't many of us, according to the admissions stats."

"Agreed," Vivian said, just as bell signaled the elevator car's arrival. "What's your name?"

"Jason."

"I'm Vivi."

"Nice to meet you, Vivi."

I'd just texted Pierre a picture of myself and the school mascot by the time the elevator doors slid open. Vivian and Jason stepped forward at the same time, and Jason jumped back.

"After you," Jason said, bowing.

Vivian giggled. I rolled my eyes, squeezing in after them.

For the rest of the walk to the Arena, I kept my eyes on my phone, managing to multitask between catching snippets of their conversation and trying to convince Pierre that he shouldn't change his degree before classes even started. Turns out, Jason is on the soccer team and was planning on meeting up with a teammate at the mixer. Pierre went to Durham University in England for microbiology and regrets his whole life—in other words, nothing's changed.

A murmur of voices and pop music rose in volume as we approached the Arena. The half-stadium featured the face of Freeman's mascot in the center of the turf, an angry red cardinal, which also happened to be North Carolina's official state bird. I tucked my phone into the pouch of hoodie as we stepped onto the turf. There was a table set up with some kids in orientation tees serving ice cream, and about a hundred first-years dispersed around the stadium in small groups.

I turned in the direction of the ice cream, but a boy stepped in front of me, blocking my path. Of course, I'd almost forgotten—with new people come new problems.

But this looked like the good kind.

"Jason, what's up?"

The boy smiled at me, and I stepped aside so he could pull his friend into a bro-hug. He was attractive. Shaggy brunette, bright green eyes, actually acknowledged my presence.

"Hey, Eric." He gave him a heavy slap on the shoulder. "How were tryouts?"

"Not bad," Eric responded. "Coach likes me enough."

Jason snorted. "Well, he hates me. Talk about advantage."

Vivian kept on a toothy grin throughout the exchange. Jason put a hand on her shoulder.

"Eric, this is Vivi. She's from Sacramento."

She extended a hand toward Eric, and he took it lightly in his, holding it there. "Vivi from Sacramento," he said, bowing a bit toward her. I almost expected him to kiss her palm. "Hello."

Part of me wanted to pretend I needed to vomit and bail the scene, but those green eyes—fuck. They found me again and kept me there.

"And who are you?" Eric asked, releasing Vivian's hand. She and Jason glanced over their shoulders at me just long enough to remember my presence before turning back to Eric. "Like the hair. Purple's my favorite color."

He had that smile back on his face again, and I found my own lips mirroring his.

"Thanks." Wow. "I'm Kathleen. Kat for short."

What a fat fucking flirt.

"Kathleen's my roommate," Vivian added, twirling a finger through her hair. "We're in Cane Hall."

"Oh, sick. So are we," Eric said, his eyes lighting up even more. "Which floor?"

"Fifth."

Jason elbowed his buddy in the ribs. "So are we," he repeated, raising an eyebrow.

I felt my phone vibrate in my pocket. As much as I would've loved to stay, calling for an ice cream break didn't sound like such a bad idea. So did leaving them to their threesome.

"I don't know about you guys, but I'm gonna get some ice cream," I said, throwing up a peace sign as I started to back away.

Just as I turned around, a heavy arm draped across my shoulders.

"Ice cream sounds good to me," Eric said, pulling me along. "I mean, it's an *ice cream* social. Why else would we come here?"

"No other reason," I replied.

The grin forming on my lips must've looked maniacal to anyone passing by. If Vivian was firing a glare at my back, I couldn't feel it under Eric's biceps. We stepped into line, his arm still hanging over my shoulder. His fingers started toying with a lock of my hair.

"So where are you from, Kat?" Eric asked. Thanks to Pierre, I was used to boys hanging around my neck, but this felt different. He didn't say my name like an afterthought or a courtesy. He *sounded* it out. Savored the taste. "Let me guess. San Francisco? L.A.?"

"Raleigh." He had my kind of sense of humor. Dry and judgmental as hell. "Right by here. You?"

"Jersey."

"Ah." I snickered. "The dumpster of America."

"Whoa," he said, pulling away from me. "According to who?"

"Everyone who's passed through it to get to New York," I laughed, looking up at him as he shook his head.

"Maybe they have a point."

We were up next in line. I asked for a chocolate cone. The girl scooping my ice cream looked like a sophomore or junior. She hadn't made eye contact with us since we'd approached—it was obvious this was a paid gig. She handed the cone over to me.

"And what would you like?" she asked Eric.

Eric leaned toward her, his arm still around my shoulders.

"What's your favorite flavor?"

The girl blushed and smiled at him.

Everything that happened on that last day—that one, beautiful last day—came barreling back to me. I saw it happen all over, felt it happen, felt *him*. Elliot. I didn't forget him. I couldn't forget the things he did. I couldn't.

"Strawberry," the girl replied.

Eric winked at her—might as well have written down his number. "Strawberry it is."

She scooped his ice cream into a cone, putting a few extra dollops on top. She handed it to him. "You're cute, freshman," she said, returning his wink. "Now scram."

Eric licked his ice cream as he pulled me away from the stand, steering me back to his group of friends.

He'd really just flirted with another girl with his arm around my shoulder—and I'd let him. Just like I'd let

Elliot and his friends kick me around, play with me, hurt me.

Of course I'd fallen for a player. So damn quick, too. I needed to get a grip.

"There's a party Friday night," Eric whispered, leaning into my ear just as I tried to break away from his grasp. "You should come."

"Why?" I responded. "You barely know me."

He saw an emo girl with a good body and thought she'd make easy prey. What he didn't see was the years of torment. Once he found out who I really was, he'd drop me like a hot fucking potato into the shadow of some other thirsty brat. I didn't deserve that. I was through with boys and their bullshit.

"I want to know you," he said, his arm dropping back to his side. He took a big bite out of his ice cream. "That's how you get free scoops, by the way."

I looked up at him. He was beaming like a kid.

How cruel.

"Wow," I laughed, shaking my head. "Is that what that was?"

"It's all that was," he said, nudging me with his elbow. I gathered in a deep breath. Fine. I'd trust him. He was no Elliot.

We arrived back at the group, and while we'd been gone, it looked like they'd picked up a new recruitment to join the posse. Giggling along with Vivian was a girl with pin-straight black hair and short-shorts. Like Vivian, she wore a crop top, showing off her belly piercing.

Jason lifted his chin at Eric as we rejoined the circle. The new girl stopped her chatter and gave me a side glance before my roommate fell back giggling into her shoulder. I wasn't stupid. They were laughing at me.

I couldn't give a damn.

"So," I said, raising my eyebrows at Eric. "Where's this party?"

Vivian went still like a deer at the sound of footsteps, ready to hang onto Eric's every word. I could see the rage in her eyes. She'd give me a verbal beating later on, a hundred percent.

"Oh, well," he said, "there's a frat house up at Powell. Since it's the first party of the semester, they're gonna let in freshmen for a limited time only." Jason caught his eye. "You should all come," he added.

"Powell obliterated our team last year, man," Jason laughed. "Booze is the least they can do for us. Count me in."

The name finally clicked. Powell University was a couple miles away from Freeman and earned the reputation of our fiercest rival, sports-wise and in almost every other niche. Students who applied to Freeman also apply to Powell, myself being the exception. The two administrations hate each other's guts.

Eric looked at Vivian. She dragged her tongue along her bottom lip.

"Sounds fun," she said, sharpening her gaze on me. "Why not?"

I ignored her look, turning to examine her new friend.

"What about you?" I said, deciding to be bold. "What's your name?"

She gave me a nauseous half-smile. "Luna," she sighed, like answering me took effort. "I'm dying to get drunk. Fuck this dry campus."

Right. If there was one distinction between Freeman and Powell, it'd be the party scene.

"Sweet," Eric said, taking out his phone. "Let's exchange numbers. We can meet up beforehand. Pregame."

I took out my phone, turning it on to find Pierre's text. One hour ago.

Don't change too much, Kitty Kat.

I swallowed. Even if I was thousands of miles away, he still had my back. He knew the real me. Maybe I wasn't much of a partier, but people change. They have to. If I wanted to start over, I would have to change too.

Once we'd all passed around our phones, Eric clapped his hands.

"So, I'm gonna go take a nap," he said, and looked at me. "See you tomorrow?"

I smiled. "We'll see."

He gave me another light nudge before turning around. I watched him go, slurping the ice cream out the bottom of his cone like he couldn't give a crap in the world. I liked him. It was official. And maybe—just maybe—he liked me, too.

2

We were going to meet up to head over to Powell at nine. I told Eric I'd miss pregaming.

Vivian had left about an hour ago, so I had the room all to myself to get ready. I almost wanted to call up Pierre and as him for his advice on an outfit, but he'd disapprove. Left to my own devices, I came up with a black tank-top tucked into my silver skirt, and two-inch black combat heels. My hair, I pulled back into a high ponytail, letting my purple curls fall over my right shoulder. Not bad for my first real party.

I checked the time on my alarm clock.

Taking in a deep breath, I grabbed my phone and a twenty-dollar bill and stuffed them into my purse. Looking at my reflection in the mirror, I felt my heart beat faster. I couldn't believe I was free—saying high school was overrated was a huge understatement.

It was all over. I could relax, begin again.

Starting now.

I opened the door to find Vivian leaning against the wall, running her mouth at Luna. As soon as she noticed me, which took longer than it should've, she hurried to the door.

"Thank *God* you're still here," she squealed, pushing past me into the room. "I totally left my room key in here. Oh, there it is." She jumped out just as quickly as she'd charged in, stuffing the plastic card into her bra. "Ready?"

"Yeah," I said, shutting the door behind me. "Where are the guys?"

I could smell the alcohol on her even as she and Luna strode about a yard ahead of me. The RAs must've not given a fuck, or were out on their own pre-classes drinking sprees.

"They're waiting in Jason's car. Don't worry, he's sober driving. Someone else will give us a ride back," Vivian answered.

Jason, sober? I barely knew the guy, but his name and demeanor were all I needed to know that the idea was impossible.

Still, I couldn't bail now.

Taking the same route as we had the day before to get to the mixer, I looked out for Tara's door. It was beautiful. She'd added some pink and blue dye to some of the edges of the gardenia petals, and leaves formed swirls and spirals around each flower from the top of the doorframe to the floor. It looked like the gateway to a fairytale. That girl was an artist, no doubt.

We crowded into the elevator with a few other girls. Once we had gotten to the ground floor, the elevator doors opened to a mob of students dressed in a combination of pajamas, business suits, strapless dresses and sweaty sports uniforms. We wove our way out to the front quad, where a car sat idling on the road near the exit. They blasted music as we approached the car.

"Can you turn that off?" Vivian yelled as she yanked open the backseat door. Jason, in the driver's seat, turned it up a notch. As we squeezed into the back, he shut it off. "Jesus."

"Sorry," Jason said, faking a pout. "I hate displeasing the ladies."

Eric sat in the passenger seat. He caught my eye in the rearview, but glanced away. The butterflies that had engulfed my intestines evaporated. Something was off.

Jason thundered up the motor, and the car crept through the streams of students dashing across the windshield before turning onto the main road. Vivian started talking up a storm as per usual, and Luna sat back in her seat, applying some dark lipstick.

"What do you think, Kathleen?" Vivian asked, turning to me.

"Um." I shook my head. "Sorry, I wasn't listening."

"I said, would you rather be called a slut for the rest of your life, or a whore?"

I raised my eyebrows. What stimulating conversation.

"I've been called both for pretty much the past four years, so," I began, pausing to let out a sigh, "a slut, I guess?"

"I second that," Eric called. I couldn't help but giggle.

Vivian shot him a look.

"Hey, Jason," she said. "How far are we?"

"Fifteen minutes."

"Great. Roomie, I have an idea." Almost turning her whole body, she faced me. "Let's play a game. It's called, 'I Think, You Think'. First, I say what I think is true about you, and then you reveal if it's really true. Then you say what you think is true about me, and I reveal my truth to you. You go first."

This *had* to be a trap—though as much as I wasn't into her first impression, she *was* my roommate. *Friends* was a stretch, but I had to make some effort to be friendly.

"Okay, uh…" I paused to see if the guys were listening in on our awkward icebreaker, but they were absorbed in soccer facts and figures. "I think your favorite food's a cheesesteak with bacon and marinara sauce on the side."

Her jaw just hit the floor.

"I'm kidding," I said, pinching back the laugher building up in me. "But not sorry."

I was a sarcastic little bitch. Couldn't help myself.

Jason glanced at us in the rearview. "What happened?" he said.

"Nothing." Vivian fluttered her eyelashes as if it were her way of dusting herself off. "Funny, but not true. My turn."

"Bring it," I said, offering a smile.

Tapping my fingers on my thigh, I waited as Vivian turned to Luna, who whispered something into her ear. Apparently this was a team sport. A couple giggles later, she turned back to me with a fat smirk on her face.

"I think you have a really sweet voice," she said, "but you're too quiet."

"Oh," I said, pretending to ignore the second half of it. "Thanks. Um, I like my voice. I don't know if it's *sweet*."

"Oh my gosh, stop." Vivian leaned into Luna for a quick second. "She's *so* cute."

Eric caught my eye in the rearview as I leaned my forehead on the window. He hadn't said a word to me since yesterday. Maybe these weren't my people after all.

"This is it," Jason said, rolling down his window. Music with a heavy bass-line exploded into the car. He gave a whoop as two boys jumped down the stairs of the house as we pulled up to the curb. "I got some friends with me, Mark," he called out to one of them.

I lifted my head off the window. "You know these people?" I asked.

"Some."

That was it. He switched off the motor and pushed open the car door. Eric followed suit and moved to pull open the backseat door for Luna to exit. Vivian followed. What a dick. Rolling my eyes, I pushed open the door on my side, stepped out of the car and slammed the door shut behind me.

It was a small two-story house from the fifties, nothing special for a North Carolina suburb. Fairy lights were strung around the columns supporting the porch while music blared from the open windows and let out pot fumes. It was a hot night, and a bunch of people were sprawled out on the lawn smoking and talking. They all seemed older than us, mostly juniors or seniors. Jason led us past them up to the porch.

I hadn't come to college expecting to show up with a full face of makeup and tight-fitting clothes to a party on my second day, but here I was, stepping over crushed plastic cups and bumping shoulders with people I'd never seen before. There was the cliché couple making out against the doorframe leading to the kitchen, the clique of girls dancing to the beat of the shitty pop music, and the sweat—God, it reeked, mingling with the pungent scent of hard liquor and beer.

"Fuck yes," Jason said, stopping in the center of the living room where a punch bowl sat on a plastic folding table. He grabbed two plastic cups. "Eric, you want some?"

"You don't know what they put in that, dude," Eric replied. "I'm gonna get a beer."

"Suit yourself."

Jason set down one of the cups and ladled the punch into his own cup until it reached the brim. He took a swig and coughed.

The liquor sprayed all over me.

"Fuck," I muttered, taking a step back from them. Someone yelled, and I whipped around to find that I'd stepped on a girl's foot.

"Watch it," she spat.

"Sorry." Her fault for wearing open-toe sandals.

"Dude, that wasn't cool," I heard Eric say, but his voice started to blend into the drone of music and shrieks surrounding me. "Apologize to her."

Shaking my head, I backed away into the crowd. Arms wrapped around me and I looked up to find Eric holding me in place.

"I'm sorry, he's being a jerk," he said. "Let me help you get cleaned up."

"No." I pushed past him, heading for the porch. "I'm good."

It took me less than five seconds to break out of the smog of e-cigs and bad breath and into the cloud of nighttime mist. The screen door rattled shut behind me. I collapsed against the wall of the house, taking in a deep breath. The fresh air calmed my nerves, though it probably had something to do with the scent of weed.

I stayed there for a few moments, listening to the throb of music beating through the thin wooden slats.

Four years of humiliation and hating myself because people hated me—I didn't belong at Woodman and I didn't belong here. Fuck this. I was going home.

"Hey."

I looked up from the floor to find myself face to face with a cigar.

"Um," I said, looking past it. "I don't smoke."

The boy lowered it.

"No hard feelings," he said, lighting it and taking a drag for himself. "Or are there?"

"Yeah, well," I laughed, shaking my head, "I'm guess I'm not exactly enjoying myself."

Nodding, he leaned back against the porch rail across from me. I expected him to start a spiel, convince me it wasn't that bad here, I'd get used to the sights and smells and bad manners and everything else that comes with college life. But he just sat there, blowing on his cigar, studying me.

I shrugged, settling back against the wall. "There's this friend of mine," I started, then rolled my eyes. "Well, not a friend. You know what I mean. He's just being a jerk, then turns around and pretends to care." I laughed again, but at myself. "I'm not making any fucking sense."

The boy took another drag, and I watched as the smoke blew out into the dark air. "Freshman?"

I waited for him to elaborate. He sipped again at his cigar.

"Yeah," I replied.

He nodded, taking a moment to rest his hand against his thigh. "Why do you think he's pretending?"

The question—his whole *demeanor*—caught me off guard. Ten seconds ago, I was ready to hitchhike my way back to campus, and now I was getting a free therapy session by long-haired dude smoking a blunt.

I mean, I'll take it.

"Because he was a different person twenty-four hours ago," I answered, pawing my boot at the splintering floor. "He was nice. Now he's ignoring me. I don't know. Whatever. It doesn't matter."

"I disagree." The guy chuckled, and his chuckle turned into a raspy cough. "Obviously this matters a lot to you." He was at the end of his cigar and crushed it into the stone column beside him. "I like to give people the benefit of the doubt. Give this jerk a second chance."

I sat on his words for a moment, then pushed myself off the wall.

"Okay," I said, backing up to the door. "Maybe you're right. Thanks... uh..."

"Kenny." He gave me a salute. "Anytime."

With that, I swung open the door and held it open for a stumbling couple before diving back into the drunken mania. Maybe Pothead Kenny was right. There was a reason for everything. Just because Eric had been acting weird on the ride here didn't mean I had to hold some petty grudge.

I'd just go see what's up.

The stain on my top had almost dried out, and no one seemed to notice it as I squeezed between the clumps of sweaty and heavily perfumed bodies. At last, I ended up back at the punch bowl table where I'd abandoned everyone.

I looked around the space and saw Luna standing in a corner with some guy, giggling like an idiot. Mustering up my breath, I went up to her, and tapped her on the shoulder. She turned around, her red lips falling into a line.

"Hey, sorry to bother you," I said in the *sweetest* voice I could, "have you seen Eric around?"

She nodded to the kitchen, then turned her back to me without a word.

"Okay, thanks!" I peeped, turning around. Bitch.

So he was in the kitchen. I pushed my way out of the living room, almost getting caught in the middle of a pillow fight. When I poked my head into the kitchen, it was empty except for a girl gagging in the sink with the supervision of her friend.

"Jesus," I muttered under my breath, reaching for my phone. "Where *is* this motherfucker?"

Hey, I texted Eric. *Where are you?*

I sank down against the kitchen doorframe, staring at the screen for two, three, then five minutes. Nothing.

Sorry I pushed you away, I tried. Another couple minutes, and no response.

I looked up at the mass of bodies swaying, jumping, colliding and falling against one another, and got to my feet. Before I knew it, I was back at the punch bowl, serving myself a clean sixteen ounces of fruity liver damage.

"Fuck it," I muttered, and knocked it back.

It came flying back out my mouth.

I bent over the floor, raking the nasty taste off my tongue with my teeth and slammed the cup back on the table. Picking strands of hair out of my mouth, I straightened back up, and headed toward the staircase.

Should've heeded Jason's gag as a warning.

I clutched the rail of the staircase and started climbing to the second floor. I'd already come all the way to this shitty party—the least I could do to make it up to myself was check the upstairs for the one who got away.

The music became a muffled merge of synths and screams as I stepped into the narrow hallway. There were only four doors, and one of them had to be a bathroom. More of the frat guys must've lived in the basement.

The first door to my left was open a crack. I moved toward it and peeked through.

The closer my face came to the wood, the clearer it became to me that someone was getting a little too lucky. Rolling my eyes, I pulled away from the door, and was about to head back downstairs when I heard a voice.

"Fuck, Vivian." I froze.

It wasn't.

It couldn't be him.

Something sick inside me—envy—caused me to crouch back down next to the door and steal a glance through the crack.

It was him.

Eric.

His body rose and fell over bed covers that weren't his, in a girl that wasn't me. Her stream of hair quivered over the mattress edge. His grunts were punctuated by her gasps, that high as fuck voice that only blonde sluts could fake.

Purple's my favorite color.

Bastard.

I ripped myself away from the door and dashed down the stairs. I wasn't shocked, to be honest. She was his type, and he was hers.

As tears filled my eyes, all I saw was his face, green eyes, stark white skin, jaw sculpted like a statue's. Elliot, Eric—they were too good for me. They were always too good for me.

Tearing my ponytail loose, I pushed my way through the crowd and onto the porch, desperate for air. Before I could slam my back against the wall again, tears rushed down my cheeks, sharp against my skin like hot iron.

Most of the smokers and hippies were gone—only a few hung around in a tight circle sharing a joint on the lawn. The night was pitch black and freezing. I hugged my arms around my chest, struggling to take in another breath.

This was what I got for taking advice from a pothead.

"Kat?"

The world stopped.

I felt nothing—not the cold current of the wind, or the moisture on my cheeks or the tightness of my top.

Wiping the tears away from my eye, I turned to look to my side.

Him.

Elliot.

He was leaning against the side of the house on the opposite end of the porch, just like me, swishing a bottle of beer around in his hand. His hair had gotten a bit longer over the summer, but his amber-green eyes had stayed the same, cutting into me as he smirked.

He'd gotten a lip piercing.

"Wow," he said, and let the word hang in the air there between us as his eyes traveled from my skirt to my bare shoulders. That one word, that one sound, was the second word I'd heard from him since that last day—and the first was my name.

My name.

Fuck, it sounded good.

"I didn't know you went to Powell," Elliot said, his gaze staying in mine.

I had to suck in a breath of air before I could reply.

"No, I…" I said, laughing a nervous, weak laugh. "I'm at Freeman."

Elliot nodded and took a swig out of his bottle. Casting my gaze back at the ground, I rolled my eyes. My love life was a mess. There was no point in sticking around. I couldn't do this all over again. I just couldn't.

After leaning my head back against the wall again, I let out a heavy breath and moved to head down the porch steps. Jason had said it was about a fifteen-minute drive. Walking for a little longer wouldn't kill me. In fact, I needed the fresh air.

"Where're you going?"

I stopped and turned to look back at him. "Home."

Elliot pushed himself away for the wall and wandered toward me. He was already taller than me, but as I stood on the first step below him, he towered over me like a deity, and I had to raise my eyes high just to look at him. He raised his hand, and slowly, reached out to stroke a lock of my hair, and twisted it around his finger.

I swallowed and glanced toward the dark street. He dropped the lock of hair so that it rested across my shoulder, leaving me cold.

"You're not walking back alone, are you?" he said, as if he was reading my mind. The gentle tone of his voice made me stare back at him. He'd never spoken to me like that before. Like he actually cared. Like he saw me as a human being. "Cause I could give you a ride."

I looked down at the bottle in his hand. Elliot rolled his eyes.

"I had, like, two sips, I promise," he said, his voice lowered to a whisper. He started walking down the porch steps, his shoulder brushing past mine.

Biting my lip, I snuck a glance back at my phone. No texts from Eric. Nothing from anyone else.

What choice did I have?

Elliot tossed the bottle onto the lawn as he walked onto the sidewalk and waited for me. After hesitating a moment, I followed him, keeping a fist curled at my side.

I'd do anything for this motherfucker. I really would.

But each time I've looked at him, I saw fangs hidden by a sexy grin, heard toxic words that sounded sweet, and gazed into soulful eyes that guarded a treasure trove of dirty thoughts. I hated him and he hated me.

This was different.

When I looked at him now, it seemed as if he'd forgotten who I was—and who he'd once been.

Elliot led me to me to a car about a few yards away from the house, parked along the curb at a slant. He unlocked it and slid into the driver's seat. I tugged open the door and brushed away some crumbs before settling down into the passenger's side.

As he revved the engine, something occurred to me. I waited until he pulled into the street, then asked, "Where're your friends?"

He snorted.

"Leo's drunk as fuck. Felix tried to go down on some chick and left her sobbing," he said, shrugging.

"So…" I said, drawing my eyebrows together, "they're at Powell, too?"

"Yeah. We're roommates."

I looked out the window and let out a breath. All three of my high school bullies lived fifteen minutes away from me, and would continue to do so for the next four years. How did this happen?

Elliot stopped the car a traffic light.

"Yeah," he continued, "none of us wanted to go too far from home. Plus, rooming with three's cheaper, so."

I couldn't speak.

I'd left high school that day thinking I'd never see them—*any* of them—again. Freeman was supposed to make a new life for me. I didn't want to know anyone, I didn't want anyone to know me.

I was supposed to be safe.

As if sensing my train of thought, Elliot rolled down his window to let in a burst of cool air. Breathing it in calmed my thoughts, and I closed my eyes as I rested my head back against the seat.

Maybe I deserved this torture.

"Hey, you know what," I said after a moment, "you can just drop me off here."

"What?"

I kept my eyes shut. I couldn't look at him. Could barely breathe.

This wasn't supposed to be happening.

Not again.

"Just pull over," I said again, facing the window.

To my relief, the car glided over to the curb. We idled there in silence as I gazed out the windshield at the black, empty road. After a minute, Elliot turned off the engine. We fell into a deep silence, but inside, the blood was screaming as it rushed through my chest. Elliot rolled down his window the whole way and dangled his arm outside it.

Part of me wanted to go—shove the car door aside, and get on my way without even slamming it shut behind me. But I was frozen, my mind was reeling, and fear kept me there. I'd be stupid to go walking out into a street past midnight in a town I didn't know, in clothes that made me feel like the whore everyone from my high school believed I was.

Drawing in a deep breath, I turned to gaze at Elliot. "Why are you doing this?"

He kept his eyes ahead of him, drumming his fingers on the side of the car door. "What do you mean?" he muttered.

He wasn't mocking me. His voice was low, serious, maybe even irritated. His lip piercing glinted in the light of the street lamps that filtered through the windshield. This time, he wasn't smirking.

How could I say it?

Why are you being nice to me? Why are you helping me?

It sounded pathetic.

"You know what I mean," I said instead, my eyes falling to his neck, tracing the black ink of his tattoo. "You're not fucking with me."

He laughed. "Don't need to anymore."

The statement hit me like a slap in the face.

I'd always figured there was a reason Elliot and his friends messed with me in school—I was smart, I had a crush on him, I hung out with a geek. But a lot of girls at Woodman were smart, and almost all had a crush on him. His words made the brutal four-year stint feel like it was arbitrary. I was an object, a plaything. A distraction.

It was for no real reason.

"So, what," I said, my voice shuddering a bit, "you've found someone else to pick on?"

He turned his head, finally looking at me. *Really* looking at me.

"I remember it, you know," he said, his breath clouding out into the freezing air like smoke as he broke the silence. "The things you said. And did."

Again, he reached his hand out to me, and I went still as it came near my chin, his fingers hovering along my jaw. Even though he wasn't touching me, I could feel my face burn.

"I could ask you the same thing," he murmured, his eyes following his fingers as they tucked some hair behind my ear. "Why, after everything I did, you were still obsessed with me."

I parted my lips to reply, but let out a small gasp as his hand touched my knee. It's not like I had anything to say. He began massaging around it in small, slow circles as he leaned toward me, and I smelled his scent—alcohol mixed with roses and ginger. Hot breath, hot sweat.

He didn't move any further, just looked into my eyes, held me there.

"If you want," he said softly, "we can pick up where we left off."

My heart pounded in my ears. All I could see was his eyes. I'd already melted into them, already given myself to him long, long ago. Obsessed. He was right. I was obsessed with him. This was what I'd always wanted.

I nodded a small, almost drunken nod.

That was all he needed.

Elliot unbuckled his seat belt and leaned forward, all in one swift motion as he kissed my jaw, and dragged his teeth down my neck.

I felt paralyzed.

He kissed me at the base of my neck, and his hand traveled up the inside of my thigh. I shivered all over. I grabbed him by his hair to tug him over to my side, but was way ahead of me—he'd climbed over to my side of the car and straddled me, pinning my head back to the headrest as his teeth continued nipping at my neck.

This was it.

What I wanted.

And fuck, it's what I *needed*.

His cock pressed through his jeans, rock-hard. I ground my hips up against him with a punching force and felt his bulge press into me. He leaned his back against the dashboard, smirking at me.

His expression just made me angry.

"Fuck me already," I breathed, and moved to claw off his jeans.

This was four years of pent-up sexual tension, held-back tears, boiling rage. I wanted it out, all out, into me. Giving him a hand job hadn't been enough to end things. This was the real goodbye. I was done with the old Kat.

I was done with him.

He put his hands behind his neck as I undid his zipper, and he laughed as I struggled to wrestle it off of him. His laughter only increased into a fit of snorting giggles after I'd failed to tear the fabric off of him.

"What's wrong with you?" I snarled.

He started pulling off his pants.

"You're funny, Kat. You're just funny," he said, still quivering with laughter. "Seems you only get horny when you're angry."

"Fuck you," I said, tugging off my skirt. The words didn't come out harsh. I almost smiled with him, but kept my lips shut, as if that would protect my fragile pride.

Once we were both in our underwear, Elliot tightened his legs around me as he leaned forward again to lick at my collarbone. The bulge in his boxers was so damn hard—it might as well have been inside me, my pussy already spilling, ready for him. Fuck. I needed him inside me.

"Why were you crying?" Elliot asked. The question caught me off guard as he murmured it, still sucking on my shoulder.

"What?" I said.

"You were crying when you came out onto the porch," he said, sitting back to look at me. "Something must've happened."

My first instinct was to respond, *Why do you care?*

I sighed, rolling my eyes.

"It was nothing," I said, but as the words left my mouth, I heard Eric's grunts, Vivian's gasps, saw it happening all over again in front of my eyes. "Nothing," I repeated, sniffling.

Nothing at all.

Elliot didn't press the subject further. Slowly, he leaned forward until his forehead was resting against mine. My thigh tingled as his hand moved along my skin and reached my soaked panties. With that one slight touch, pleasure rocked through me. My legs flexed wider.

He looked at me, and I nodded.

Elliot slipped a finger underneath the fabric. The contact made me feel like I was struck by a bolt of lightning as he sifted through the coils of my soft hair. I gripped him by the shoulders, and my back arched up from the seat as he slipped another finger into my panties.

Just because I'm a virgin doesn't mean I intend on staying one.

The words shot through me as he plunged his finger up my vagina.

I let out a seething gasp, and Elliot met my gaze, waiting to continue. Bucking my hips to give him my answer, I forced his finger farther into me.

"Fuck," I breathed, pressing my head into his chest as he started fingering. "Elliot."

He was starting out slow, sinking his finger in and out of me, a little deeper each time with a calmness that proved he'd taken the virginity of girls hundreds of times before in this car. He knew what to expect, he knew what to give to me, and how to give it.

But I knew what I could take.

"Fuck me," I practically spat, looking up at him with cloudy eyes. "For real."

Elliot shook his head. "Don't have condoms."

"Don't care," I said, taking his wrist and pushing his hand harder against my opening. "Do it."

"I can't," he murmured, leaning against me. He plunged his fingers harder into me, and I quivered as he kept up the pace, thrusting faster and deeper into my throbbing pussy. My thighs felt like they'd melt right off my bones. The heat of his chest, his breath hot against my neck, his fingers pounding into me—all pure ecstasy.

Then it happened.

Heat gushed out my opening. Musky sweetness filled the air. It felt like the wind was knocked out of me. I collapsed back against the seat, my eyelids fluttering as my body relaxed. Elliot slipped his fingers out of me and raised them up. They were glistening with my insides, and he wiped them casually on his discarded jeans.

I remained there, motionless, watching as he climbed back over to the driver's seat and gathered up his jeans, leaving me with my legs outstretched, panties half-tugged down my ass, sweat leaking down my thighs.

Glory.

That's what this felt like.

Elliot didn't look at me as he pulled his jeans back over his legs.

Exhaling, I pulled up my panties and felt around on the floor for my skirt. We straightened ourselves out in silence and Elliot started up the engine. We didn't speak a word as he drove me back to campus, dropping me off at the precise spot where Jason had parked his car just a few hours ago.

Before I stepped out of the car, Elliot put a hand on my shoulder, and squeezed it. That was all. I couldn't care less. Once he'd pulled away, leaving me with my head spinning, standing in the cold, that's when the smile came. Shaking my head, I turned to head back into the dorm.

Eric could go fuck himself.

I was over it.

3

The next morning, I woke up thinking about him. It'd all started in ninth grade. My parents had just gotten a divorce the summer before, so my dad moved away while my mom and I stayed in Raleigh. I hadn't cared at the time, still don't. The dude was a jerk, not a father.

We weren't poor, solid middle class if anything. I was always a goth, loud-spoken, unafraid of expressing myself and my thoughts. Whether it was through the color of my hair or the swears flying from my lips.

In ninth grade, I'd met Elliot. And everything had changed.

I rolled over in bed to check the time on my alarm clock. 10:40 AM. Lifting my head up from my pillow, I scanned around the room for signs of life from Vivian. Her half of the room was just as demolished as before, if not more so. It looked as if she'd shed her outfit the second she'd returned for the night, a small pool consisting of her clothes and purse discarded at the door.

I closed my eyes again, and my thoughts turned back to him.

Elliot was different from people like me and Pierre. Physically charming, likable in seconds, the kind of kid that doesn't need to dish out compliments in order to make friends. I'd watched him from afar for months. Maybe he'd known at first, maybe he didn't. I hadn't been obvious about my feelings for him.

Then one day, I'd bumped into him while walking down the hall at school. It was the first time I'd really looked into his eyes, that he'd acknowledged my existence.

I lifted the sheets off of me and slid my feet onto the carpeted floor. I sat there for a moment, looking at the soft light filtering in through the cracks of the window shades, glossing over my desk and vanity.

I didn't know what it was that I saw in him—maybe a flicker of warmth in those eyes—that kept me drooling over him for years, even after he'd stripped me down, humiliating me in front of the whole school, spread vile rumors about my dad, forced Pierre to do his homework and did everything else under the sun that's stereotypical of a high school bad boy. Maybe it was just his pretty face.

His friends had been the worst part.

If it'd just been Elliot, I could've socked him in the jaw every time he threatened me, no problem. But he always had company. Even if they weren't manhandling me or shooting glares in my direction, they had the moral support of an entire school body ready to snicker and gasp at my slightest moments of embarrassment.

The school administrators were another story. Elliot and friends had rich parents who had friends, and friends of friends, who ran the scene around Woodman. Even if I'd reported Elliot, the security guards would more likely shut my mouth than come to my rescue. It'd sucked, but after months of the same shit, I'd learned to deal with it. I'd learned not to let it get to me.

Despite their massive trust funds, Elliot and his gang just so happened to end up at the same shitty kind of public university that I did.

Some luck I had.

I felt the urge to erupt into spitting laughter as I dragged myself out of bed to pull on some clothes.

Kathleen Silver, you're a piece of fucking gold. It may have taken me four years to prove that to myself, but it was worth it in the end. Last night couldn't have been real. But it was.

I was capable of facing my fears.

Once I'd pulled on a T-shirt and some shorts, I reached for my phone. Apparently, I hadn't been the only having the best night of their life, either.

My roommate came in at 3 and vomited all over the fucking place, Pierre had texted me. *How was your night?*

This time, I didn't resist the urge to chuckle to myself. I couldn't give a shit if my laughter was going to wake up Vivian. She deserved some lost beauty sleep.

Honestly, I began writing, *not as shitty as I thought it'd be.*

I'd leave it at that.

After brushing my hair and clasping a few bangles up my arm, I slid on my boots, grabbed my room key, and headed out the door. The hallway was completely still and quiet, which worked for me. I wanted to get a head-start on finding my classes before the coursework started to actually pile on. As I walked toward the elevator, I pulled up my schedule for the semester on my phone, and began reading through the list. First class of the day was at eight.

I entered the elevator, punched the button to bring me to the ground floor, and blew out a long breath as the doors squealed shut in front of me.

Eight. Okay. I could survive that.

The doors opened to the lobby, and the scent of Lysol and fresh coffee fought over my senses as I stepped onto the tile floor. There were a few students out and about, some heading to the dining hall for a late breakfast, and others, like me, up to scout out their professors and classrooms before the school year officially began.

No one said a word to me as I passed by the front desk toward the door, not that they had to—I didn't recognize any of them. A couple of girls running the desk watched me as I pushed through the door. Glancing over my shoulder, I could've sworn I saw a couple of them snicker.

Well, bitches will be bitches. I wouldn't be surprised if gossip had already made rounds through this stupid love triangle that consisted of me, Eric and Vivian.

The quad was far more energetic than the inside of the dorm. A lacrosse team was meeting at the far end of the lawn, a group of boys sprawled out on benches and blasted music, groups of girls milled across the patios surrounding the grass. A few boys tossed a frisbee back and forth across the whole landscape while an elderly lady pushed a stroller along the perimeter. I started cutting across the lawn to reach the first building.

Even though I wasn't alone, there was something calming about being surrounded by tons of people I didn't know. It gave me space to think, without having to think about what everyone thought of me.

My mind strayed back to Elliot.

Suddenly, I felt the tremors back between my thighs, his hands all over my shoulders and through my hair, the smoothness of his voice.

Seems you only get horny when you're angry.

I hadn't been angry. I'd been dead serious.

When I'd first heard his voice at that party, I'd thought I was dreaming. Fifteen minutes. That was all the time that separated me from him, my past, the person I used to be.

It was thrilling. And terrifying.

The first building was the oldest on campus, and also one of the smallest, with brown brick walls, and stone steps leading up to wide, wooden doors framed by a set of white columns. A picture of modest academia. I started up the steps and held open the door for a couple of faculty making their way out of the building before stepping inside.

The door squealed as it swung shut behind me, and the sound echoed throughout the long hallway. It was empty, aside from a student chatting with an adult in front of one of the doors. I checked the room number on my schedule and headed into the stairwell to the second floor. I reached the classroom, snapped a photo of the door and went back outside on the quad. One down, five to go. The number of people that had been lazing around on the lawn had multiplied by a dozen. A gaggle of girls—had to be freshmen—scooted past me on cruisers, and it looked as if a ten or so more students had made the boys' game of frisbee into a tournament.

My next classroom was located in the building right next door. I trekked toward it, and the group of cruisers steered around me.

"Oh, shit," one of them called as they sped past.

They glanced at me over their shoulders and continued on without another word. Narrowing my eyes, I peeked behind me. There was no one else there.

Shaking my head, I walked up to the next building. As I pushed through the revolving door, I heard someone let out a whoop from behind me. I turned around just in time to see two boys pointing at me just before I was forced into the lobby.

What the hell?

I stood there, watching the boys through the glass as it rotated to a stop, until they continued on past the building.

Maybe I was imagining things.

No.

Something was wrong.

Instead of going ahead to find the room, I stepped back through the revolving door. I'd probably just put my clothes on inside-out, or something stupid like that. The students here may have been enrolled at a university, but they still had the basic sense of amusement as toddlers.

I crossed the quad again and heard more snickers coming from behind me. Whipping around, I saw a couple students angling their phones at me. Taking a picture, no fucking doubt.

I started to walk faster.

More heads turned in my direction as I passed. Some girls pointed at me, laughing. A couple guys covered their eyes, some fanned the air in front of their noses. I forced my eyes to the ground.

In shorts and T-shirt, was I still too emo for them?

What the fuck was going on?

I was jogging now, pretending to ignore the side-glances and gestures. But my legs were beginning to tremble. I couldn't take it. It was only my first day at Freeman.

This had to be a dream.

"Kathl*ee*-een," I heard a familiar voice call. Vivian. I waved her off, hoping she'd get the memo that I wasn't in the mood to talk. "Catch!"

Something smacked my butt.

"What the hell?" I muttered, whirling around.

A tampon lay on the ground in front of me. I looked up. Instead of Vivian, Luna stood a yard away in the company of Jason and Eric. She must've adopted Vivian's voice like a fucking bird call. Jason was bent over in laughter. Eric hid his smile behind his hand, staring right into my eyes. I looked back at the tampon.

It all clicked.

I twisted around to look at the back of my shorts, and there it was. A big, red splotch of blood.

"You've got to be kidding me," I seethed. My cheeks flushed, and I started backing away from them, trying to tug my shirt down over the stain. But it was huge, so there was no point in trying to cover it up. Gritting my teeth, I looked back up to find Luna sobbing with laughter, phone out, poised toward me.

"Very funny," I yelled at her, not caring that a few people turned their heads to watch the drama.

If someone—especially a girl—ever caught me bleeding out the back of my pants, I'd expect them to exhibit a little female solidarity and kindly *tell* me, not turn it into some pre-teen joke. Was that too much to ask?

I turned around to speed-walk back to the dorm building and took the stairs back up to my room. Keeping my head ducked down, I managed to avoid more stares. Finally, I was able to shut the door behind me for some privacy. Vivian was sitting up on her bed, scrolling through her phone.

"Morning," I said, in a forced little sing-song.

To my relief, she didn't look up as I strolled across to my side of the room and began rifling through my duffel for a new pair of shorts.

"Hey," she replied after a long moment. Obviously hungover.

I managed to kick off my soiled shorts, pulled out a new pair and fresh underwear, then felt around in my bag for some pads.

Something in my bag caught my eye.

I reached into the bag and lifted out a pair of skinny jeans. The back of it was stained bright, period-blood red. I took out another pair. Stained.

And another. And another.

"What the fuck?" I whispered, dumping out the entire contents of my bag onto the floor. All of my pants, shorts, skirts, were stained red at the back, as if I'd sat into puddles of red paint every day of the week for the past year.

Paint.

Dropping the clothes to the floor, I turned to look at Vivian. She was watching me, her hand covering her mouth. She snickered.

"Did you do this?" I asked, more shocked than angry, as if the fact that she was capable of doing anything like this wasn't processing in my brain.

Of *course* she'd do something like this.

"It's just a joke, Kathleen." Vivian fell back on her bed, hiccuping in laughter. "It's *ketchup*."

"Just a joke?" I said softly, then put on a tight grin. I crossed my arms. "These are the only clothes I have. You *knew* that."

"Relax," she said, hopping off her bed. She rushed over to me, grasping my shoulders. "We were drunk, okay? We got some fries and stuff after the party and had all these leftover ketchup packets. We thought you'd find it *funny*."

"Well, I don't," I said, raising my voice, and broke away from her hold. "This stuff's never going to come out."

Did this girl *have* a brain?

You don't just take someone's only spare change of clothes for three whole months and dump a gallon of condiments over it.

You just... don't.

As I turned my back to her, the tears came bubbling up and out of me, and before I knew it, I was raking at the box of tissues on my vanity. Vivian kept silent as I wiped the snot from my nose and crawled onto my bed. Digging out my phone, I shot her a livid glance.

She didn't seem the least bit remorseful. A smug little smile remained on her lips.

"Come on, Kathleen," she said, cocking her head to the side as she took a step toward me. "It's *just* a *joke*."

"Well, your *joke* is going to cost me money." I tossed the tissues onto the floor and flipped onto my back, staring at my phone. "Unless you're willing to go shopping for me."

Vivian let out a huff and twirled back on her heel toward her side of the room. No? Yeah, thought so.

Getting mad wasn't worth it. The silent treatment was good enough. I didn't want to deal with her petty excuses. Drunk, dumb, whatever it was that had convinced her it was okay to ruin my wardrobe, it didn't matter. The damage had been done.

I found my mom's number and began to text her. After a moment of struggling to string the words together to justify needing to wire a couple hundred dollars more into my debit card, I paused.

If I told her that I needed money for new clothes, she'd ask why.

Throughout high school, I'd managed to keep the already high-strung single matriarch unaware of what was going on at school. I knew for a fact that she was already worried about my moving away, even if it was just an hour's drive from home. Last she'd heard, I was fine. Protecting her sanity would protect mine.

Who said I couldn't keep up the act?

Drawing in a breath, I laid my phone face down on my chest and stared up at the ceiling. I was still in my underwear. Asking my roommate to borrow some shorts was out of the question. Closing my eyes, I wracked my brain for one person, any *single* soul, on this campus that I'd actually had some sort of an alliance with.

Tara.

Getting out of bed once again, I pulled my soiled shorts back on, reached for a sweatshirt and tied the sleeves around my waist so that the cloth concealed my behind. Avoiding Vivian's gaze, I strode back across the room and entered the hallway, letting the door slam shut behind me.

Drawing in a breath, I walked over to Tara's door, and knocked. A few seconds later, I heard the sound of feet shuffling across the carpet, and the door cracked open. Tara peered out at me like a rabbit afraid to leave its hole, until I smiled at her.

"It's me," I said. "Kat."

"Oh my gosh," she laughed, opening the door for me. "Sorry, I've been having a weird day. Come in."

"That makes two of us," I said, letting out a tired laugh as she ushered me into her space. I looked around, my eyes drawn to the string of lights and Polaroid photos that formed a canopy across the ceiling. "Wow."

"Thanks," she replied, grinning.

My eyes fell to her bed, which was unkempt, but made up with sheets in bold colors, then moved to the flower pots at her window sill. There was only one bed, one desk, one vanity.

"Where's your roommate?" I asked, turning to face her as she closed the door behind us.

"Don't have one." Tara's grin only grew wider. "So, what's up?"

I raised my eyebrows as I looked around again at her clean, artsy setup. I'd kill to be her roommate.

"Well, this is random, but..." I let out a breath. "Do you have any pants, or shorts I can borrow for, like... two days?"

"Of course, but ..." Tara nodded, moving to her closet. She looked genuinely concerned. "Can I ask why?"

"Yeah," I said, with a long sigh. "Sorry. It's kind of a stupid story. My roommate and her friend poured ketchup all over my clothes to make it look like I bled through them, and—"

I paused as Tara bit her lip, hiding a smile.

"It's kind of funny," I said, mirroring her grin. "You can laugh."

"No, it's not," she said, shaking her head. "It just ... wasn't what I was expecting."

I shrugged. "That's Vivian for ya."

Tara went still, squinting at me just as she was about to reach into her closet. "Vivian, right," she said. "I know her."

"You guys went to school together, right?" I asked.

"Yeah." The word was sharp, as if the word *school* had unearthed some searing memories. I knew the feeling.

She must've realized how she'd said it, because she glanced back at me with a nervous grin. "Sorry. We weren't close or anything, is all."

"Let me guess," I began, tapping my fingers against my chin in an exaggerated gesture, "this period prank thing isn't totally out of her comfort zone."

Tara shook her head and moved to her bed to lay out a few pairs of shorts and jeans. "She's done worse, believe me."

I felt a pit form in my gut as I watched her fold the clothes into a neat stack and gather them into her arms. Even though I'd spoken to her just once before, she was kind enough to lend me her own clothes, almost no questions asked. It was obvious that she had a bitter past with Vivian. It made me angry to think that anyone as sweet as her could be a victim of high school drama.

"Here," she said, handing me the bundle. "Keep them as long as you need."

I smiled. Even though her eyes were dark, there was light her gaze.

"I can't thank you enough, Tara," I replied, turning toward the door. "Seriously."

"No problem," she replied, shrugging.

"Would you want to get dinner tonight?" I asked, just as I was about to open the door. "I mean, if you're not busy," I added, surprised at my sudden willingness to take our acquaintanceship to the next level. Tara's eyes brightened even more.

"Sure," she said. "Actually, I was going to invite a friend over for board games if you want to join after."

I nodded, smiling. "Sounds good."

"What's your number?" Tara asked, pulling her phone out of her back pocket.

The plan was to meet up at seven to head down to the dining hall, which I'd been avoiding since yesterday out of fear of being seen nibbling alone in some dingy corner of the packed place. We exchanged info, and I let myself out of her room with a silly smile on my lips and good vibes in my gut.

I'd made a real friend.

Before turning to walk back to my room, just out of curiosity, I peeked into the lounge to find a kid flipping pancakes on the stove as he chatted to girl sprawled out on the couch. They seemed chill, my kind of people.

Maybe I could build a life here.

Leaving them in peace, I continued down the hall, and paused in front of my door as I heard footsteps behind me.

"Hey," said a familiar voice.

Eric.

I turned to see him coming down the hall, and he slowed his stride as he approached, sticking his hands in his front pockets. He tried smiling at me, but when I didn't reciprocate, he lowered his gaze to the floor. He stopped in front of me.

"You want me to let you in, or something?" I almost hissed at him, trying to mask my voice in sarcasm. "I'm not Vivian's butler. You can knock."

He ran a hand through his floppy brown hair.

"Look, Kat," he said, "I'm sorry about yesterday."

I waited for him to explain. As far as I knew, he hadn't realized that I glimpsed his little rally with Vivian the night before. That wasn't my business. If he was apologizing for ignoring me, then that was another thing.

He'd invited *me* to that party. Not the other way around. The least he could've done was greet me in the car. Follow me out to the porch, make sure I wasn't getting raped on my way home alone. That is, if Elliot hadn't become a godsend by offering me a ride back.

Elliot.

I shook the thoughts away. Last night was a one-time thing—my attempt to prove my own self-worth by going after what I wanted, by getting the last laugh. That was all. I could never forget the things he'd done to me.

"I didn't come here to see Vivian," he said, stepping closer to me. "There's something I need to tell you."

"I'm kind of in the middle of something," I said, hefting the bundle of clothes in my arms. He'd just fucked my roommate in front of my eyes not even twenty-four hours ago. I didn't want to hear whatever was going on inside his head. "Can it wait?"

"I like you," he said.

Huh.

Now this was interesting.

Stuffing the clothes under my arm, I leaned back against the wall opposite of him, and stayed silent.

"Look," he said again, blowing out a long breath. He mirrored my stance as he stood back against the wall. "I think you're really cool. And nice. And… I guess I'm just not used to girls like you."

I nodded, as if permitting him to continue. I'd be lying if I said I didn't like what I was hearing.

"I want to get to know you better," he continued, cracking a lopsided grin. "Maybe in a less distracting setting."

"What?" I said, laughing. For someone who seemed like the stereotypical jock that most girls drool over, he wasn't the smoothest talker. "Are you asking me out?"

When he avoided my gaze, and the question, I knew exactly what he'd meant. It wasn't that he was bad at talking to girls, it was that he never had to in this way. He never had to commit—it was all lust. Vivian was just another dose of that drug.

I knew exactly who I was dealing with.

And kind of enjoyed it.

"Just…" He shook his head, pushing himself away from the wall. "Think about it. Okay?"

"Okay," I said, watching him go back down the hall and turn on his heel as he ducked around the corner. I turned back to the door, and was about to press my key card against it, when his head popped back around the wall.

"Just so you know, I don't like what she did to you," he said, looking at the clothes in my arm. "I'm sorry."

With that, he disappeared, leaving me with a warmth turning in my stomach. Taking in a deep breath, I unlocked the door, but before I could enter, it swung wide open.

Vivian was on the other side, hand on the handle, just as she'd done the first day.

"Oh, hey," I said.

When she didn't move, I tried to shoulder my way past her. When she didn't budge, I plastered on a wide smile, just in case she didn't get the message. Her eyes were boring into mine.

"Excuse me," I tried again.

"Just so you know," she said, her voice so calm that it scared me, "if you try anything with him, I'm going to make your life hell."

Woah.

I blinked back at her, still registering her words. So, she'd been eavesdropping. What a dirty little bitch—and she'd said it as if she wasn't making my life hell already.

The nerve.

"I'm sorry, but," I began, "Eric sought *me* out, just so you're aware."

A wicked smirk rose and fell on her lips as quick as a flash of lightning. It said, *I don't care.* I felt a cold rush down my spine.

This was all too familiar to me.

I was different from her. I was a threat. She held power over me in her looks and toxic disposition, and she'd only exercise it over me as long as it kept her afloat, kept her above me. Just like Elliot. Just like Felix. Just Like Leo.

I couldn't repeat high school. I couldn't face four more years of cowering, hiding, tip-toeing around eggshells and still getting hurt, bearing the brunt of some egotistic rich kid's wrath. Something had to change.

"If you try anything," she said, her frigid gaze unmoving from mine, "you're going to regret it."

Elliot fucking Lancaster. Of *course*.

If anyone knew what it'd take to get rid of someone like Vivian, it'd be the king of torment himself.

Vivian's gaze darted between my own eyes, trying to figure me out, trying to locate my weak spots from the outside-in. Something told me that even if I *didn't* try anything, she'd still do everything in her power to make my life miserable. I couldn't let her get to me. Not this time.

"You're on."

4

I'd spent the last hour holed in up my room, my finger hovering over the *send* button.

It hadn't been hard to find him. Elliot Lancaster was the first user that popped up in my Instagram search history—and I felt no shame. His account was public, so after scrolling through photos of him shirtless at the beach and rugged selfies with his buddies, I'd drafted a vague little message and pasted it into his DM.

Point blank, I was asking him for help. With what, I wouldn't specify, not until we spoke about it in person. Even if Elliot had grown out of his bullying phase over the summer, I didn't want to risk more evidence of my desperation going viral.

I closed my eyes and counted to three.

When I looked at my screen again, I clicked.

The message was sent.

I flopped back onto my bed, pressing my phone against my chest as I looked up at the ceiling. It was more coated than the walls of bathroom stalls at Woodman, but tamer. The white tiles were speckled with tributes to moments of young love scrawled in Sharpie, partially washed out hearts and names next to the occasional *Fuck this school* or *Follow me @...*

My phone vibrated. I lurched upward, sitting on the edge of the bed as I looked at the screen.

U free now?

That was all. Quick reply.

Again, I closed my eyes, breathed till the count of three and texted back, *Yeah.*

I looked at the time. Vivian had gone for lunch with Luna. If Elliot wanted to see me now, I'd either have to go trek the thirty minutes back to Powell, or he'd have to come here. Even if Vivian was gone, I didn't want to risk her showing up in the middle of our scheming against her.

My phone vibrated again. I swiped the message open like my phone would explode if I didn't.

I can pick u up in 10.

There. No questions asked.

Elliot was coming to whisk me away from my dorm and back into his world—not quite high school, but his own territory, nonetheless.

My heart already was beating like it was on fire.

I took in a couple drawn-out breaths as I rolled off my bed to pull on some shoes. The deep breathing was supposed to remind me that my visit was for one purpose, and one purpose only—use Elliot to my advantage, not the other way around.

The warning signs were clear. Dousing all my clothes in ketchup was all the fun Vivian needed to have for me know that if I didn't do something, I'd have to endure more harmless "jokes" for the next ten months. I'd gone down this path before, saw where it took me, and didn't want to go there again. Ever.

I was going to break the cycle, but I couldn't do it alone.

A few minutes went by as I paced the room until a car horn honked from outside. Narrowing my eyes, I peeped through the window blinds to see Elliot's arm hanging out the window of his car, just like the night before. Even though there were multiple cars parked out there, he honked again, as if there weren't a hundred other kids waiting for rides of their own. He didn't have a care in the world.

I grabbed my purse, room key, and glanced in the mirror before heading out the door. Thankfully, Tara and I were about the same size, and my shirt tucked into her shorts without hassle.

Another breath.

Okay.

I tugged open the door, veered down the hall, and resisted the urge to vomit as the butterflies increased in my stomach. As I waited at the elevator, it occurred to me that I didn't know what to say to him. After all, he'd finger-fucked me just hours ago.

Do I thank him? Mention it at all? Pretend it never happened?

The elevator doors screeched open, and I stepped into a cramped group of about five other kids.

Pretend.

I'd pretend.

The elevator jolted. Five seconds later, we all poured out into the busy lobby. Noise packed the space. Some extracurricular club was selling donuts by the doors, the students working the front desk yelled at kids to show their IDs, and a large tour group was making its way toward the stairwell. Despite the craziness, as soon as I started walking toward the doors, I could hear nothing but my beating heart.

I pushed past the glass door into the humidity of the afternoon. I could practically hear the blood pounding in my ears as I strode up to Elliot's car, casting side-glances at people as I passed them, as if I expected them to know, and care, just whose car I was about to get into in the broad light of day. That may have happened if we were still in high school, but right then, no one gave a damn. Just as well.

The front of the car was facing away from me, but I could still feel Elliot's eyes on me in the rearview as I approached the passenger side. He unlocked the door, and I slid into the seat.

"Hey," I said, keeping my eyes forward until he started the car and we rolled out onto the street.

After a moment, I looked at him. He hadn't said a word. His arm still hung out the window, the other draped nonchalantly over the steering wheel. He wore black Aviators that concealed the eyes I loved so much, a white tank top and ripped jeans. Fifty bucks said that if I hadn't texted him, he wouldn't have gotten out of bed until much later. He was that kind—live it up late, sleep when you're dead, or if you can't wait, during daylight.

"So," he said, breaking the silence between us. That one word sent shivers down my spine. "You need me."

Well, that was one way to put it.

"I need your expertise," I said, wondering how long I could dance around the subject before I needed to explain what was going through my head. Now that I thought about it, the stupider my idea sounded. Get a bully's help to confront a new bully. It'd sounded logical at first. "Since you're, you know, good at dealing with people like this."

"Like who?"

I couldn't tell if he was annoyed, or genuinely curious. His voice was deadpan.

"My roommate."

Elliot turned to look at me for the first time since I'd gotten into the car, since he'd dropped me home in the middle of the night. It was just a glance, no feeling, as if making sure he'd picked up the right girl.

"Her name's Vivian," I continued, and waited a moment to see if he had any reaction. None. "She brought me to that party last night."

Elliot let out a snort. "I was wondering how you managed to show up," he said.

The comment stung, but I understood what he meant. If it weren't for Pierre, I was one step away from flaunting the status of a loner. If Eric hadn't invited me, I would've stayed in.

"Anyway," I said, brushing the remark aside, "she's kind of a bitch. No, I take it back." My face was scorching hot. I struggled to find the words to explain. Finally, I let go. "She's like you."

"Hm."

Nothing else.

The car shook as we pulled into the gravel drive that led past Powell's front gates and into the campus. I waited for Elliot to elaborate. Instead, he cursed as a mob of students started racing across the road, and honked a couple times before revving the engine.

Once we drove past them, I looked back at him.

"Do you know what I mean?" I asked, sounding more timid than I wanted to.

"No, not really," he responded. Cold. "You're being kinda cryptic."

I shook my head. "What the fuck is that supposed to mean?"

"Exactly."

I bit down on my tongue as he swerved the car down into the parking garage and landed a spot a second later.

Elliot turned off the engine and it sputtered into silence. Then he turned to me, leaning forward as he pushed his sunglasses up onto his forehead. My insides quaked as I took a chance, looking into his eyes only to instantly regret it.

"Here's the thing," he said slowly, as if speaking to a child. "I can't *help* you if I don't understand what it is you *want* from me." His eyes were blazing, heated, beautiful. "So spit it out."

The sudden venom in his tone made something in me crack.

"First of all, fuck you," I blurted.

I slapped a hand over my own mouth. Elliot only smiled.

"Continue," he said, his eyes suddenly alive, as if he'd been dying of boredom up until this moment. "I like what I'm hearing."

Even though he tempted me with his smirk, I was too angry to give him any credit. On a normal day, he could melt my insides with that one turn of phrase, that bit of eye contact. Not now.

I was too far gone. Too fucking mad.

"Second," I continued, "it's like this. You're a bully. She's a bully. I'm fed up." Now it was my turn to lean toward him. "Tell me how to get rid of her."

His smirk only turned into a wide, bright beam. Instead of pressing the subject further, or even acknowledging what I'd said, Elliot pushed open the car door and jumped out. Letting out a frazzled breath, I stepped out after him.

"Follow me," Elliot called over his shoulder, already walking toward the garage exit.

The car beeped as it locked up, and with that, I trailed after him toward the staircase up to the ground level.

"Where are we going?" I asked, checking over my shoulder back at the stairwell landings to make sure we weren't being followed by a mob of kids bearing cameras pointed in my direction.

"My room," Elliot replied casually. "There's food there. Haven't eaten yet."

A smile flashed across my lips. I was right. He'd woken up to a text from me, and seeing me was the first thing he'd done today. I'd bask in that thought for as long as was grossly possible.

He flipped his Aviators back over his eyes as we came outside and beelined through a crowd of students toward the dormitory as if he'd done this a hundred times before. As if he already owned this campus, already had half the freshman class kissing his ass just so they wouldn't become the next Kathleen Silver.

We breezed past the front desk of the dorm building and made our way into a free elevator car without company. It didn't even occur to me until after we'd risen to the third floor that I hadn't been asked to show student identification. It was as if just by being in Elliot's presence, I was automatically enveloped in his aura, masked by the scent of his cologne and protected by the shield of his cutting gaze.

What a celebrity.

I felt my stomach drop as the elevator lifted us two, three, four floors high, though I couldn't tell if the elevator was all to blame for the sudden rush to my belly. The sensation continued even after we stepped out into the hallway, and only grew as Elliot led me down a fluorescent-lit hall, high-fiving some boys as we passed, nodding at a few of the girls, before we made it to the end.

This was his place, his world, and I was about to become fully part of it.

The door was already cracked open. Rock music belted from within. Elliot kicked the door aside with his foot and stepped aside.

"Ladies first?" he said, holding the door open for me.

Gulping, I stepped inside to find two other pairs of eyes staring at me. Felix and Leo. Elliot's henchman, bred from the same socioeconomic bubble, preened like prom kings, still the same.

Felix, Elliot's right-hand man, was his striking polar-opposite—toned brown skin complete with a splash of freckles across his cheeks, eyes almost as dark as Elliot's ink. His brown hair was faded around his ears and sculpted into a wavy masterpiece at the top of his head. Gold chains dripped from his neck and down the center of his chest.

Leo, prankster of the group, screamed pretty boy with shoulder-length blond hair swept back from his forehead like he was born soaking up sun on a surfboard, aquamarine eyes rimmed with eyelashes so dark you'd swear he was wearing mascara. *Always smirking.* But if you're like me, the words you hear coming from those pretty pink lips might as well qualify as death threats.

When they saw me, their eyes lit up. Not because they were happy to see me, at least, not in the way most boys' eyes light up when they see a girl with a half-decent face. They saw me as a game, a game they knew how to play.

"Surprise," I said lamely.

Leo hit his phone, and the music turned off, breaking the awkward moment. He sat back in his desk chair, folding his hands behind his head.

"Well, well," he said, and the rasp in his voice brought back so many, *too* many, memories. "Couldn't get enough of us, huh?"

His smile was so big and bright that it could've been flirty if it wasn't coming from the kid who'd set my hair on fire and snuck weed into my soup.

He raised his eyebrows at Felix, who lay stone-cold on the bottom bunk, staring up at me. He was more confused than anything. Obviously, Elliot had spared them of a warning of my arrival, but I doubted he'd kept our impromptu one-night stand a secret.

"Kat," Elliot began, "has a request for us."

He shut the door, turning the place into an interrogation room. I turned around to face him.

"Wait," I whispered, narrowing my eyes at him. "I didn't come here to talk to them. I came here to talk to *you.*"

He snickered, taking my shoulders in my hands, and spun me around.

"If you want my help, you're getting help from all of us," he whispered back in my ear. "Unless you've changed your mind."

I felt the anger curl back up in me again. I wanted to turn around and sock him in the jaw. Once again, he'd gotten me—he'd trapped me in a situation I didn't want to be in, with the same people who'd made my life a living tragedy. The difference was, this time, I'd asked for it.

This was my choice.

"Fine," I said, rolling my eyes.

Elliot loosened his grip from my shoulders to lean against the bunk bed ladder. A bag of chips lay on the floor and he bent down to scoop it up. "The floor's yours."

Crossing my arms, I looked around for a place to sit or stand a little less awkwardly before Felix nodded to the beanbag stuffed in the corner of the room. Hesitantly, I dragged it over to the center of the room, kicking away a dirty pile of clothes.

"So," I began, situating myself in the bean bag, "there are these girls at Freeman. They're set on making my life hell for the next four years if I don't do something."

This sucked. I hated having to plead for help, but my pride should've been the last thing on my mind. It's not like they were unaware of the past four years of my existence at Woodman.

"Who?" Leo asked. I looked up at him, expecting to see a smirk playing on his lips, holding back a snicker. But he sounded genuine. "Upperclassmen?"

I shook my head. "My roommate. And her friend. And maybe," I paused, rolling my eyes again as I thought of Jason spewing punch all over my top, "her boyfriend."

"So that's three people," Leo continued. "Sounds familiar."

"I know," I said flatly.

Felix sat up in his bed and swung his legs onto the floor. "What *exactly* do you want us to do, Pussy Kat?" he drawled, reaching up to snag a few chips from Elliot's bag. "Give 'em a spanking?"

I couldn't help but snort. "That'd be nice."

He looked at me and gave an amused smile. It was mutual. For once, he wasn't laughing at me. He was smiling *with* me.

It was a weird feeling.

"Seriously, though," I said, dropping my gaze, "I need you guys to find a way to get rid of her. Switching rooms isn't enough. She's... how do I explain this..." I sighed. "She thinks I'm going after her fuck buddy. She'll push me out of this school if she gets the chance."

I looked around the room to gauge everyone's reactions. Elliot stood still against the bed frame, except for his chomping, squinting at the floor as if deep in concentration. Felix had his hands folded in his lap, his gaze also concentrated on the floor. Leo had dropped his arms back to his lap and had slumped back even farther in his chair, watching me.

Maybe I'd been expecting a couple snickers or side glances, but there was none of that. They were waiting for me, politely, to continue.

Odd.

"I can't let her get to me like..." I sucked in a long, tight breath. This was so hard. "Never mind. You know how get under someone's skin. Teach me," I said, staring at Elliot. "Teach me how to stand up to her. Tell me how to win."

Elliot met my eyes, but it wasn't he who spoke first.

"I'm in," Leo blurted, raising his hand. He looked at Felix. "I mean, I'm still kinda confused as to what you want us to do, but whatever it is..." He jumped up from his chair and took a slow step toward me. "I'm sure we can make it happen."

He winked and whirled around to snatch the entire bag of chips away from Elliot. I felt a little flutter of warmth within me.

"Dude!" Elliot exclaimed, and rolled his eyes as he slouched back against the bed, "Whatever."

"If I had to guess," Felix began, "she wants us to teach her how to be one of us, so that she can iron out some drama." He looked at me, and his dark eyes sent chills down my spine. "Isn't that it?"

I nodded, shrugging my shoulders. That was one way to put it, sure. In other words, I wanted them to help me preserve what little pride I had left. How ironic.

Both Felix and Leo glanced at Elliot, and so did I. They needed his final word. After a moment of waiting for his input, I felt the butterflies in my stomach morph into pins.

"You know what," I said, pushing myself out of the bean bag, "this was a stupid idea. I should go."

I should've known this was a trap, if anything. A joke. They *loved* having me come here to plead for their assistance, like I was truly some slut in need of saving. Once again, I was their puppet, and because I'd been trained by their hands, there was no doubt I'd fallen back into their game simply out of muscle memory.

It was sick. *I* was sick.

What happened in high school should've stayed in high school.

I put my hand on the door handle and yanked the door open. Just as I was about to step outside, I felt a hand on my shoulder. The touch made me freeze.

"Kat," Elliot murmured. I let go of the door, and it glided back into place. "I know exactly what you want."

His hand lingered on my shoulder, and slid down my upper arm, letting go just before it became too much. I turned around to face him, and instead of looking into his eyes, my gaze fell on his soft, almost pink lips.

"Just get rid of her," I forced out. "I can't risk leaving school. I'm not running away. Please."

I waited for him to respond, but a smile spread on his lips. I swear, if I got down on my knees to beg it'd make him cum on the spot. He loved this. He was *enjoying* this desperation.

Maybe I could milk it in my favor.

"I'll do anything," I said, raising my eyes to his. "Just do something."

He seemed to like what he heard. Maybe that was the only acknowledgement we needed, the only reminder of last night, of our time along together. Bending down, his lips came close to my ear.

"We'll do to her what we did to you," he whispered. He sounded serious. Too serious.

I stepped back from him. I wanted to get a good look at his face—at *all* of their faces. Out of the three of them, I'd expect Leo to be the one bending over in snickers at witnessing our little moment. But they were all serious, as if the prospect of hurting someone who hurt me was actually up their alley for once.

Elliot *must've* told them. About us. About last night.

"Really?" I asked, just as the answer revealed itself in my own thoughts. "You're going to help?"

Could it be that—

"I like you," Elliot said, with a shrug. He reached up to my face and took a lock of my purple hair, twirling it around his finger.

He started pulling it down.

"Just kidding."

"Ow!" I swatted his hand away as my scalp stung. "What was that for?"

"For nothing at all, sweetheart," he said, smirking. His words dripped with sarcasm. He was crazy. *I* was crazy for doing this. *I like you.* More like, *I like it when you're weak,* and I'd go along with it if it got me what I needed.

"So?" I said, shaking off his remark. "You want me to pay you? Because I doubt you need the money."

Rather than snort, or roll his eyes, laugh, do anything else, Elliot flinched. He glanced over his shoulder back at the other guys, and leaned back against the bed frame, giving me room to breathe.

"You're right," he responded. "That won't be necessary." He gestured toward Leo and Felix. "What should this tradeoff be, fellas? This is a group matter, after all."

Felix raised his head toward me.

"I think we should give it a minute," he said. "Whatever it is we do to this girl, it should match whatever Kat does for us."

"So, we wait," Elliot said, beaming as turned toward me. "I do love some good sexual tension."

Leo cracked a grin.

"Well, cool," I said, pretending to have missed that comment as I turned to leave. "Thanks, guys. I'm just gonna—"

"You need a ride?" Leo asked, taking a step closer to me. "'Cause I could bring you back."

"She has a ride," Elliot said, almost a little too harshly. He must've realized how he sounded because he cleared his throat and wiped his palms on his shorts—as if sounding possessive himself made him sweat. "It's fine. Come on, Kat."

I raised my eyebrows at Leo as Elliot held the door open for me. If I were to be honest, I wasn't used to the whole sudden bout of chivalry. Didn't think they were capable of it to be honest. But hey, I wasn't complaining.

I nodded to Felix as a goodbye, but he'd reclined back on his bed and was scrolling through his phone, as if I'd never invaded their space to begin with. It was obvious he wasn't thrilled about all of this.

Couldn't blame him.

We ducked back out into the hall. This time, Elliot kept a fast pace, and before I could register just how queasy I felt about all this, we'd crammed into the elevator and were gusting down to the garage level. We made the awkward journey without a word.

When the elevator doors parted, I decided to break the silence.

"So, what happened to you guys?" I said, deciding to be a little cocky. "Puberty?"

He shot me a look. "What're you talking about?"

"The whole nice-guy thing," I said. "Deciding to go along with this plan. A couple months ago you guys were kind of, like, total dicks, to put it lightly. Is this a facade?"

Elliot tossed me a goofy grin, and I felt those butterflies knowing at my lungs.

"Whatever it is," he replied, "enjoy while it lasts."

What a fucking jerk. Cute, too.

No. Stop.

Taking in a deep breath, I picked up the pace after him as we approached his car, and slid into the passenger seat without managing to look at him. The problem was, I could already feel my cheeks flush. Sure, I was done with Eric. I was done with Elliot. I was done with my past—but my feelings said otherwise.

And... so did Elliot.

"What's this bitch's name, anyway?" he said, turning on the engine.

"Vivian," I replied. "Russo."

"Hm."

Elliot stretched his arm out over my headrest, twisting around as he backed the car out of the parking spot. I tried to ignore the fact that his face was so close to mine, that his fingers brushed past my hair as held onto the back of my seat. It just lasted a moment—thank God—before he shifted back into his seat.

"So," I said, drawing in a shaky breath as we pulled out of the garage and into the bright light of day. "What are you going to do with her?"

Elliot smirked at me through the rearview.

"You don't need to worry about that, sweetheart," he replied, nonchalantly draping his arm back over my seat as he turned onto the street, steering with one hand. "The question you should be asking is, what am I going to do with *you*?"

I looked at him. He was still grinning that close-lipped grin of his, mischievous, hot, and so damn punch-able. Maybe, after all these years, I'd been wrong. He didn't hate me. None of them hated me. They liked me for who I was—which would be their source of entertainment. I was Elliot's drug, his love-hate relationship, and he pushed and pulled at me to stave off his boredom.

My quest for sanity was his joy ride.

"Yeah," I said, after a silence that was longer than it should've been. Like I cared. My heartbeat was throwing sparks. "Do something about my new bully, then I'll consider the possibilities."

"Deal."

5

By the time Elliot had dropped me off, it was around four in the afternoon. I had enough time to take my signature Kat nap, chill in my room for another hour or so, then start getting ready to meet up with Tara for dinner.

Feeling gutsy, I was putting some mascara on when Pierre pinged. I reached for my phone and scrolled through the screen. He'd been texting me while I was with Elliot and the boys, and I must've missed his messages.

Fuck my life, he'd written. *Classes just started and I'm already failing.*

I giggled and started to write back.

That's gotta be an exaggeration.

A moment later, he responded, *I wish.* I waited for him to elaborate. *How are your classes?*

They don't start until Monday. Still doing the orientation BS.

I snorted at my own reply. In other words, still squeezing out the last bouts of teenage angst. And then some, in my case.

But he didn't need to know that.

Ah. He'd left it at that, and so would I.

Switching off my phone, I placed it on the vanity and turned my attention back to the tube of mascara in my hand. Heavy eye makeup wasn't foreign to me—I'd been made fun of because of it in middle school, complimented because of it in high school, and abandoned it altogether these past few weeks. I hadn't wanted to give off the wrong sort of impression to my future college peers.

Too late.

I put down the mascara wand and picked up the eyeliner. My phone pinged again. This time, it was Tara.

Hey, she said. *Want me to come to your room?*

I heard a knock at my door before I could type back. That was fast. Shrugging, I put down the makeup, cursed my bad time management and skipped over to the door. Putting on a smile, I opened the door.

Vivian was staring back at me, looking like she'd just got dropped into a bucket of red Gatorade. Her hair was sopping, the blonde strands washed out in red liquid, and her white top looked bloodier than a sloppy tie-dye job. I covered my hand with my mouth, unsure of whether I wanted to break out in sobbing laughter or just... gasp.

"What are you looking at?" Vivian squeaked, pushing past me as she plowed into the room and slammed the door shut behind her.

I watched as she went rifling through her disaster of a closet to pull out a large towel and a few bottles of shampoo.

"What..." I started, but she shot me down with a glare.

"Don't even bother finishing that question," she snapped, shaking the bottles. She growled. "Fuck. They're *empty.*"

I snickered. "How often do you wash your hair?"

She responded with another growl and threw the empty bottles back into the closet. Then, as if realizing who I was, she whipped around to face me, and took a slow, calculating step toward me, as if she were figuring out just how quickly she could pounce and sink her claws into me.

"This was your fault, you know," she said.

I put a hand up to my chest in mock offense.

"I'm sorry, but I'm not even quite sure *what* happened to you."

"What *happened* to me," she said through crazed, bared teeth, "was ten gallons of cheap hair dye raining from the sky onto my *head.*"

I widened my eyes, looking like I was feigning surprise more than I was feeling it.

"Oh?"

"Oh, what?" Venom could've sprayed from her lips, and I still would've laughed. "What the *fuck* makes you think you can do something like this to me, huh?"

Throwing up my hands in defense, I backed away toward the door, trying to keep the laughter from gurgling up out of my lips and vomiting it onto her. This was just too much for one day. Too *good*.

"I am being one-hundred and one percent honest with you," I said, finding my tone growing sharp. "I had nothing to do with... whatever this is."

"Oh, yeah?" She forced on the most clownish smile I'd seen in a long time and shoved her phone in my face. "Tell that to your little boyfriend."

My first thought went to Pierre, which made me grimace—who else would she be talking about? But Pierre was an ocean away, and I didn't have any other...

Oh.

She'd pulled up a video of herself shrieking as a waterfall of hair dye fell in watery globs over her head, shoulders, everything. The camera panned from her to the roof of the building above her—looked like the outside of the dining hall—where a skinny blonde boy was perched, gripping his stomach in laughter.

Leo.

"That's..." I bent closer over her phone, and almost reached out to hold the screen closer to my face, as the video replayed itself. "... not my boyfriend."

Vivian tore the phone away from me. "Yea, right. Slut."

With that, she pushed past me again and flung open the door. With the toe of my boot, I caught it just before it went slamming back into the wall, watching as she dashed down the hall and into the bathroom.

"And so it begins," I murmured, grinning to myself as I slunk back inside the room.

I closed the door behind me, and my phone screen lit up on the vanity. I moved toward it and looked at the screen to find a DM from Elliot.

Had a feeling red was her favorite color, he'd said. *I saw all the photos they posted. How unoriginal.*

I scrunched up my nose. What photos?

And then I remembered it.

All the kids, pointing their phones at me, as I ran across campus with a fake period stain. It was no surprise that he was so aware of my moments of social suicide.

Giggling, I texted back, *Thank you. Seriously.*

About a minute passed before he responded, *Thank me later.* He put a winky face. *I'll pick u up at 10.* Wow, so soon.

There was a knock at my door. For a split second, I hesitated, thinking Vivian had forgotten her room key before realizing that I'd made plans. Letting out a breath of relief, I pulled open the door to a smiling Tara. Her hair was braided and bound with colorful ribbons, and like me, wore a shimmering, shameless layer of eyeshadow. Unlike me, her look was complete.

"Ready?" she peeped, before examining my makeup. "Uh, you need help?"

"Nah, I got it," I laughed, letting her inside. "Just got distracted."

I skipped back to my vanity and quickly continued where I left off with the eyeliner. All of a sudden, I felt starving. This wasn't my first time trying the food here at Freeman, and it was nothing special, but now, it was all I could think about.

Maybe it was the ketchup.

I snorted at the thought. Tara gave me a concerned look. "You good?"

"Yeah, great, actually," I said, twisting the cap back onto the eyeliner. I was a little out of practice, but it made me feel like myself again. "I was just thinking about something."

"Ah." Tara made a slow round through my half of the room, just as I'd done with hers, inspecting the bare walls. Then she turned to look at Vivian's side. "I just saw your roommate running down the hall," she said, picking up an empty bottle of liquor from the waste basket, as if it were a clue. "She's going to have to throw this out in the back, you know. They do room checks next week."

Oh, yeah?

"She was running to the bathroom," I explained, and decided not to go any further. Some things were best kept secret. "And I couldn't care less if they catch her drinking in here. If she isn't kicked out by then, I'll shoot myself."

Or summon Elliot's wrath.

"You want to care, trust me," Tara said, dropping the bottle back. "It's either you dispose of this stuff, or she does. You might both get punished."

I shrugged, looking back at the waste basket. If what Tara was saying was true, even though Vivian might get suspended, or at least moved to a different room, that punishment wasn't enough for me. Nope. If I wanted Vivian to go down, I wanted it to be slow, painful, and oh-so entertaining.

"You're right," I said, and grabbed a jacket from my duffel. Moving toward the door, I bent over to pick up the bottle, then wrapped it up so that it was concealed. "I'll spare her. Just this time."

She had better things coming her way.

"You're too nice."

"That's what you think," I chuckled, opening the door. We went out into the hall. "I'm kidding. I just don't want to be accused for something I didn't do."

The hall wasn't as dead as the night before. Seemed as though everyone got their partying jitters out of their systems. The smell of weed floated down the hall, and as we turned, I spotted an RA barreling up to a group of boys smoking it in the corner. Clutching the jacket close to my chest, we managed to squeeze past the scene.

"Sucks for them," Tara giggled, and I joined in with her laughter as we reached the elevators. Then I remembered something, and guilt rode through me. I just had to ask.

"Do you smoke?"

Tara looked at me, raising an eyebrow high, as if she were shocked to hear that question.

"Isn't it obvious?" she said. "I mean, I'm a total hippie."

"Sorry," I replied, stepping into the elevator. "I didn't mean anything by it. It's just... after I met you, Vivian told some stupid joke about how you were growing weed under your bed, or something."

"She did?" Tara threw back her head in laughter. "That's funny. Not a bad idea, either."

"Pretty crafty, actually," I agreed, letting out a mental *phew*. "But enough about her. Who's this friend we're meeting up with later?"

"He's an upperclassman," Tara said, shyly sweeping her hair back from her face. I raised my eyebrows. We reached the ground floor, and the doors whooshed aside. "Sophomore. His name's Kenneth."

"Ooh, Kenneth," I said, lightly punching her in the shoulder. "Going after older guys are we?"

"More like the mature ones."

We entered the lobby. It was funny that we'd both felt the need to dress up our faces for a night on the campus dining hall. Other girls stood around in bunches with full faces and skin-tight cocktail dresses, as if they were heading out to clubs or bars, neither of which we were allowed to set foot.

"What's with all the glam?" I whispered to Tara.

"Sororities," she replied with a bit of contempt in her tone. "They start recruiting this evening."

I narrowed my eyes at the girls. "Really? Already?"

She blew a braided lock of hair from her face as we exited the building. "Yeah. They're, how do I put this, pretty prevalent around here."

Before we stepped outside, I turned my head to get one last glance and the groups of glittering, high-heeled students to find a few of them staring back at me. One of them snickered and whispered something to the group.

"Just throw it in there," Tara said, nudging my arm. We were standing in front of the quad now. I followed her finger as she pointed to a ramp leading to a driveway at the side of the dorm building.

Those girls hadn't been looking at me. They'd been looking at the jacket in my arms.

Was smuggling the bottle *that* obvious?

"Right," I said, quickly veering off toward the ramp while Tara waited.

Of course, I couldn't have been the only one who used the old wrap-the-bottle-in-an-inconspicuous-piece-of-cloth trick to avoid being caught. Once I reached the bottom of the ramp, I spied the overflowing dumpster container leaning against the side of the building. I walked up to it, stuffed it deep into the opening, and quickly turned to head back up to the quad as if nothing had happened, tossing the jacket over my shoulder.

"Good Samaritan, you," Tara giggled as I returned huffing and puffing from the climb back up the ramp. "Now let's eat."

"Please."

The dining hall was a straight walk across the quad, and it was pretty empty by the time we'd arrived. We piled food onto our plates and had no problem finding a couple window seats.

"So," I said, once we'd been sitting for a minute or so, as twirling a clump of spaghetti around my fork. "What exactly did Vivian do? You know, back in high school. What was she like?"

"If I tell you," Tara said, giving a comical grin, "you might get scared."

"Ha," I replied, shoving the pasta into my mouth. "I doubt it. Come clean."

"Well," she began, dabbing at a bit of dropped tomato sauce with her napkin, "I used to be friends with her in middle school. We were pretty much inseparable. But when high school started, she got prettier, and I got, well..." she rolled her eyes, "I didn't. She's been a bitch ever since."

"So she's superficial," I said. "You know, when I met her for the first time, she practically gave me a once-over. I could tell right then and there that we'd be enemies."

"Enemies?" Tara raised her eyebrows. "Wow, that's heavy."

"It's true." I took a sip of water. "She made it clear she doesn't like me, so I don't like her."

"That makes two of us," Tara replied. "No, take it back. I *hate* her."

"That ketchup prank," I said, turning to look at her. *Really* look at her. "Is that as far as she'll go, or does it get worse?"

I expected her to return my question with a smirk, or a half-assed bit of sarcasm. Instead, she replied, "She destroyed my paintings."

She kept her eyes down at her plate and took in a deep breath.

"I was an honor's roll kid. All my teachers loved me, but my art teacher, Ms. Reilly, she was the best."

She smiled as she said it, and that innocent, pure sentence made me feel a pit in my stomach. It was just like when she lent me her own clothes—it didn't make sense for someone to hurt her.

"She encouraged me to put together a portfolio and submit it to this top art school in New York. I was psyched. They were giving out full-ride scholarships for the program. I spent months working on it."

She paused, looking around the room as if realizing her surroundings for the first time. As if she were waking up from a good dream into dry reality.

"I'd made these beautiful portraits. Did some still life. You name it. Just before it came time to submit it, I'd dropped it off in Ms. Reilly's classroom so she could take a final look. When I came back to pick it up, she wasn't there, but the classroom door had been unlocked. Only two people had keys to that room—me and Ms. Reilly."

"Vivian stole it?" I suggested.

Tara nodded. "Basically. She does that sort of thing."

"How'd you know it was her?" I asked, trying to sound sensitive. "I mean, why would she do something like that, anyway? That's just… cruel."

She let out a heavy breath. "I saw her as I was heading back to the classroom and she'd told me she made, 'just a few improvements,'" she said, making a high-pitched imitation of Vivian's voice. "Improvements, my ass."

"But… why?" I just couldn't wrap my mind around that fact that even someone with a shitty sense of amusement would pick on someone like Tara. "Sorry, we don't have to talk about it. It's just—"

"She doesn't like it when someone's better than her," she said. "She can't deal with it. She's insecure, that's why."

"That doesn't excuse what she did," I said, putting a hand on Tara's shoulder.

"I know it doesn't," she said, letting out another breath. "If it weren't for her, I'd be in art school, not... this place." Tara shrugged, as if she didn't just say the most depressing thing I'd heard all week. "I guess it's hard for me to be too angry about it when I know her so well. In middle school, she was everything to me. We were best friends. I just... don't know what changed."

We fell into a solemn silence as we continued picking at our food. I imagined Vivian's face, went back over her words in my head. After she'd eavesdropped on Eric confessing his petty crush on me, she'd basically threatened to ruin my life, which was exactly what she'd done to Tara. And she'd succeeded.

I let out a sigh and glanced around the cafeteria. The dessert counter was a few yards away, and it looked like they were serving up ice cream sundaes. I nodded toward the counter.

"I think I'm gonna get some," I said, standing up to clear my plate.

"Ooh, good idea," Tara laughed, following suit. We brought our dishes to the conveyor belt of dirty plates and headed over to the dessert table. I couldn't help but think about Eric, when we'd gone to the ice cream social together. It's where a friendship had blossomed and died all at once, even if I didn't know it.

"Yup," Tara said, digging into her cup of chocolate ice cream as we headed back up the stairs to the first floor of the dining hall. For a cafeteria that conducted all its operations in the basement of a grimy building that was made in the fifties, they didn't fuck up the cooking as much as they could've. "That was so good."

"Agreed."

Moments after we stepped back outside, my ice cream had already melted at the bottom of my paper cup.

It was a nice night for a somewhat hectic day, and I took in a deep breath of warm air. The sky was a deep indigo, typical for a southern summer night, and fireflies were blinking in and out across the dewy grass of the quad. Groups of students sat stretched out on the lawn, laughing, chatting. For the first time since I'd stepped on this campus, I really felt at ease.

I felt at home.

"Hey," Tara said, leaning into my shoulder. "Why's that kid staring at us?"

She nodded to the dorm building. Standing at the foot of the stone steps, twirling a cigarette between his fingers, was Leo.

He must've been looking at me for a long time, because when I'd looked up at him, he'd already made eye contact. As soon as I saw him, he pushed away from the railing and began walking toward us.

I stopped and held my breath.

"Hey," Tara said, slowing down. She glanced back over her shoulder at me. "Do you know him?"

"Yeah," I said a little absent-mindedly, already taking slow steps past her. "Hold on a sec, I just need to…"

What was he doing here? Did Elliot send him?

"Hey," I said as we approached each other, meeting in the middle of the quad. He took a drag on his cigarette and held it up to me. I shook my head, refusing the offer. "Cut to it. What do you want?"

"What do I want?" Leo laughed, his voice deep, raspy. "Come with me, and you'll find out."

He didn't need to give anything more. Turning on his heel, he stuck his cigarette in between his lips and headed across the grass.

"Hey!" I called, but he didn't turn back. Letting out a huff, I turned around to give Tara an explanation. "Look, he's… an old friend of mine. I gotta see what he wants," I said, fumbling for the right words. "I'll meet up with you at your room. Okay?"

Tara shrugged. "Fine by me."

Letting out a breath, I left Tara's side and strode across the grass, closing the distance between me and him as I reached out my arm and grabbed his shoulder, forcing him to pause.

"Hey," I said, unsure of what I was intending on saying. Leo whirled around, smirking.

"Yes?"

Shaking my head, I let go of his shoulder and continued walking. "That was quite a feat you pulled," I replied, letting a smile slip past my lips. "Red looked good on her."

"You're welcome."

Just as we were about to cross the sidewalk that separated the quad from the rest of the buildings on campus, I asked, "Where are we going?"

He nodded to the dorm building. "You'll find out."

Whatever.

I followed him past the entrance and around the side of the building where Tara had told me to throw away the bottle. Leo speed-walked past the trash bins and over to where a fire escape wove up between the darkened windows of students' rooms and supply closets. He hopped up onto the first rung and turned around to offer me a hand.

Rule number one of dealing with Leo Borowski—always, *always*, check his eyes before taking his hand. I swear, the phrase, *eyes are windows to the soul*, was created just for him and his baby blues.

I looked up at him, and the smirk still hung beneath his wicked, glittering glance. Despite acting casual, his gaze gave it away—he had a plan, and he'd manipulate me into following through with it, one way or another.

"Your choice," he said, as if reading my mind. "I can only guarantee you won't die."

"What exactly are we doing?" I said, laughing a bit. I couldn't help but cringe at my own reaction to his vague words.

"Come on, scaredy-Kat," he said, grabbing my wrist before I had the chance to back away, and pulled me up the steps of the fire escape.

My heart jumped a little, and I bit back the fear in me as I followed him up the flimsy steps, gripping the handrails of the ladder as if I'd fall into something much worse than a flat sheet of concrete.

"So," I called, finding that he was a couple yards up ahead of me. It took all my restraint not to glance down, and thrill alone motivated me to continue climbing after him. "Whose idea was it? Yours, or Elliot's?"

"Are we still talking about drowning your roommate in a vat of hair dye?" he called back. Even twenty feet below him, I could hear the smirk in his tone. It made me shudder with excitement.

"Of course, we are."

"That," he began, pausing dramatically to glance down at me, "was what we like to call a collaboration. A little more effort on my part then Ell's, obviously."

"Obviously?"

"I'm the one who had to perform the parkour and pour the shit," he said matter-of-factly. "I assume you saw the footage."

I snorted. "Yes, I saw the footage of you laughing your ass off."

"And you didn't?"

The image of him rocking back and forth in hysterics and Vivian's sopping-wet dog hair flashed before my eyes. I grinned, imagining how it must've looked from above the cafeteria roof.

"I am now," I chuckled, shaking my head as we continued up the fire escape. A breeze blew past, and I clung tight to the rails like a cat to a tree trunk. "Hey," I called up to him, shutting my eyes, "are we almost there?"

I felt a hand on my shoulder and sneaked a peek to find Leo squatting before me. I was holding on inches before the edge of the roof and felt dumb as he offered me his hand. I moved to take it, but hesitated, and even went so far as to lower myself one rung down.

Why was I doing this?

Why did I want to be near him?

He'd been the sole mastermind behind the many "harmless" jokes and pranks that Elliot and his boys pulled on me throughout our years at Woodman. This wasn't the first time he'd faked being the nice guy, the spontaneous charmer, before turning his back on me for the sake of tragic comedy.

Maybe I was a little afraid.

And I had every right to be.

"What are you doing?" he asked, sounding more hurt than anything else.

I shook my head, taking another step down.

"This isn't safe," I lied, to which he responded with another raspy laugh.

"And you didn't realize that five minutes ago?" He reached down again, but instead of going for my hand, he stroked my hair. "God, you're a wimp."

So maybe he hadn't lost his gritty humor entirely.

"Come on," he said, pouting. "Is anything safe really that fun?"

I sighed. So it's one or the other.

I heard Elliot's voice go through my head. I did have my own end of the bargain to hold up, and Leo had come through. Vivian was knocked down once—no doubt, she'd come back with full-throated revenge.

I'd agreed to this, hadn't I?

"Fine," I said, grasping his arm. He pulled me up, and I rolled onto the rough surface of the roof. Luckily, it was completely horizontal, like a large cement plateau, so my fear of sliding down to my doom was subdued for now.

"Well?" Leo said, stepping back and spreading his arms wide as if talking to the whole world. "What do you think?"

His bright blue eyes landed on me, waiting. I turned to focus on where he was pointing. Below, students milled in and out of the buildings and relaxed across the dark grass. Even from up here, I could see spurts of fireflies, and the creaking sound of doors opening and closing felt familiar.

"Nice," I said, turning to him. "You got me. I'm a typical girl who likes pretty sunsets. Now what's the price?"

His eyes seemed to grow even wider, and he let out a short laugh. "You're funny. How about a peck on the cheek?"

I stepped closer to him. "And?"

"And we'll go from there," he said, his voice turning serious all of a sudden, as if he were negotiating a drug deal, or more likely his grade for a pass-fail class. "Whatever I want, right?"

"Those are the rules," I said, biting my lip as I turned my head to gaze out at the distance. I thought of Pierre, and Tara, and my mom. My life was severed into two—a vicious cycle so filled with love and hate it could've been a Shakespearian rendition. My inner circle, people I cared about, wouldn't accept my behavior if it had come from anyone else but myself.

I couldn't ignore that side of myself, the side that was screaming out *this isn't right.*

This isn't *you.*

But I'd agreed to this. At some point in my past, this is what I'd wanted. I had to follow through.

"Actually," I said, sucking in a deep breath as I took his hands in mine. "It's whatever I want."

I yanked him forward. His lips crashed against mine, and I could feel him squirming to get away from me. Instead of relenting, I sunk my tongue deeper into his mouth, put all my weight into that one, deep kiss before pulling away.

I wiped my arm across my mouth. Leo stared at me, frozen like a statue caught seconds before getting rammed to the curb by a passing car on the freeway.

Here was the thing.

I might've agreed to that little contract of give and take—but just because I didn't make up all the rules didn't mean I had to follow them blindly. Elliot and his crew could pretend I was their plaything all they wanted, but I was done succumbing to the stereotype they'd created of myself. They may have drawn those bounds, but I'd surpass them. I wanted to be in control.

This time, I would be.

"Is that what *you* wanted?" I asked, dragging my tongue along the rim of my lip, tilting my head to the side. "Because that's what I wanted."

I replaced my arms over his shoulders, holding him there.

"Or was it this?"

I ground my hips up against his and immediately felt a reaction—hard.

Looking up to meet his gaze, I smirked, finding his expression still struck frozen, like he'd been flashed by a ghost.

Yup. I'd stay two steps ahead of him.

"I—" Leo gulped. It was the first time I'd ever seen him at a loss for words, and it only made my smile spread wider. "I thought you were a virgin."

"And?" I almost spat back. "That could end at any time, couldn't it?"

He opened and closed his mouth a couple times before letting out a nervous laugh. "Then I guess that makes two of us."

I stared at him.

"Wow," I said, backing up for a second, putting my hands on my hips as I turned around, and ran a hand through my hair. Then I turned back to face him. "I don't give a fuck."

With that, I grabbed him by his shoulder with one hand, and moved the other to his ass. I couldn't help giggling a bit as I squeezed it, finding it firm, round like some fucking balloon. For me, it wasn't about the sex. It wasn't about the superficial transaction of my body for his protection. This was the first time in many ways, but most of all, it was my first time I was dominating my dominator. And it felt good.

I smashed my lips back onto his, my teeth tugging at his lip.

"Damn, Silver," Leo breathed, breaking the kiss just long enough so that our lips brushed together as he spoke. "I didn't know you were this thirsty."

"Shut up," I whispered, taking his hands in mine again. I moved them to my shirt. "Make yourself busy."

Lifting my shirt just high enough, I let him slip his hands over the curve of my bra, and shuddered as his cool fingers made contact with the skin just beyond the fabric. He paused for a moment as he looked into my eyes, as if waiting for the okay to continue.

"What are you waiting for?" I reached down to unbutton his pants. "I got somewhere to be, just so you're aware."

I felt his pants tighten between my fingertips as his own hands moved over the mounds of my breasts, carefully squeezing, massaging them, feeling them like he was fumbling through the dark to find his way. I'd already undid his fly, and the bulge of his dick pressed through his boxers.

I pulled down the elastic slow enough to irritate him. He put more pressure on my breasts, dipped his head to my collarbone, and began sucking lightly at my skin. His blonde curls were soft against my skin, and his cheek was warm against my own neck, slick with sweat.

Just as I was about to go in for his dick, I felt something vibrate in my pocket.

My phone.

My first thought was to ignore it, but suddenly, Leo slipped it out of my back pocket. Before I could protest, he'd answered the call, pressing the phone up against his ear as he stepped away from me.

"Yo," he said, just as I tried to yank the thing away from him.

"Leo!" I hissed, trying to refrain myself from kneeing him in the balls. "What the fuck? That could be my mom, or something."

He pulled away farther from me, my shirt falling back into place as he spun around and stuck his free hand into his back pocket. He wandered around the roof, putting on an air of sarcastic confidence, as if he'd just called up some hypothetical executive, or an ex-wife.

"Uh-huh. Yup. Nope. Sure. When? Now? Hold on," he said, and looked back at me. "It's Elliot."

I strutted toward him, holding out my hand.

"Hand it back to me," I said, "before I slap you."

He raised the phone back to his lips.

"She said she's gonna slap me," he said, raising his eyebrows at the stupidly sexual innuendo. I'd given up. A series of muffled curses came from the phone, and Leo held it out toward me. "I think he's mad."

I snatched the phone from him and put it to my ear.

"Hey."

"Where are you?" Elliot said from the other end, sounding like he was talking through a tight jaw. "Why are you with him?"

I glanced back at Leo. He simply zipped up his pants as innocently as could be done. He knew the fun was over. I turned my back to him.

"When you said I have to do whatever you guys want," I said slowly, lowering my voice, "I assumed that applied to, well, all *three* of you."

"It does," he ground out.

"So?"

I could hear him let out a hard breath, and then, "You were supposed to meet me thirty minutes ago."

My first instinct was to roll my eyes and hang up on him, but I lowered the phone from my face and checked the time. He was right. It was way past ten—more than thirty minutes.

"Just come," he said, and the line went dead.

I let out a sigh and slipped my phone back into my pocket. Turning back to face Leo, I was met with his goofy grin.

"He's jealous," he said. "Greedy bastard."

"I doubt it," I muttered, turning back to the fire escape. If anything, he was sexually frustrated and I was his easy way out.

I made my way back over to the fire escape. Before crouching over the ladder and lowering my foot down, I glanced back at Leo, my gaze snaking up his tanned calves and resting on his white T-shirt. Didn't even get to feel what was beneath it. Shame.

If anything, *I* was frustrated that we had to be interrupted. I wasn't lying when I said that I wanted to call the shots.

I'd wanted this.

I'd wanted him.

Maybe it was just for the thrill of it. Some superficial reason, something primal, something to do with my inferiority complex. I didn't care. The second I was about to get what I wanted, Elliot had found some way to interfere.

So be it.

If I was to survive this, I'd have to roll with the punches.

I gripped the top of the hand rails and lowered my left foot down onto the first step.

"See ya," Leo said, puckering his lips and blowing a kiss.

"You're not coming down?" I asked, imagining him crouching over the edge of the roof, stalking every person who walked by beneath us for the sole sake of judging each and every one of them. If he had nothing to do, that would definitely be his default course of action.

"Nah," he said, batting his hand at me. "Imma stay up here a bit."

"Suit yourself," I said, smiling as I descended. "Weirdo."

Just before my head dipped past the edge of the roof, I stole a quick glance back up at him to that he was still standing there, watching me. His gaze had softened.

"You're cute," he said.

"I know," I replied, though it came out sounding more like a question. He chuckled at my sudden awkwardness. Shaking my head, I continued climbing. I wanted him to say it again—*you're cute*. Just to make sure I'd heard him right.

Bitch.

Loner.

Slut.

He'd called me all sorts of things, even came up with a few colorful names of his own that I couldn't remember—but never *cute*.   Never anything remotely positive, nothing close to a compliment.

This wasn't respect, but it was something.

Going down the fire escape took a lot less time than it did going up, and I even hopped down to the ground past the last couple of rungs and ran back around the corner of the building, past the trash collection bins and up the ramp to the main campus. I tried, unsuccessfully, to smooth out my hair as I headed around the dorm building to the driveway. It was dark, except for the street lamps and screens of cell phones glowing against students' faces as they wandered around the parked cars.

There, Elliot's Mustang sat rumbling at a rough angle to the curb, as if he'd tried parking and re-parking a few times before giving up. Like before, his arm hung out the driver's seat window. The second I started approaching the car, I saw him twist his head to watch me. He didn't even bother using the rearview.

"Hey," I said, pulling open the passenger-side door and sliding into the seat as if I'd done it a million times before. In retrospect, it felt like I had. "Sorry, I—"

He pulled me toward him, and my lips met his. The kiss was fast, but deep. He pulled away first, leaving my head to almost fall into the crook of his neck, and left me feeling almost tipsy.

"Wow," I said, blinking as I reclined back into my chair.

Did he *know* how much power he had?

"Let's get the fuck out of here," he muttered, revving the engine a few times before pulling out of the driveway and out onto the street.

"Where're we going?" I asked, a little more breathlessly than I would've liked. This was way too much action for one night—but I wasn't exactly complaining.

He pulled over the car almost as soon as we'd left the campus, parking smack in front of an enormous house.

White columns, clipped hedges and everything. I recognized the atmosphere right away—even though all the windows in the car were rolled up, I could hear the pulsing of a beat drop that define most shitty pop hits these days. But as Elliot pushed open his car door, it became clear to me that this wasn't just any party.

"Come on," he said, and ran around the side of the car to open the door for me. "I'm going to show you what a real party looks like."

I felt that tug in my chest again, my nerves telling me that something exciting was on the horizon. I was at the top of an emotional roller coaster. The tipping point.

I stepped out of the car.

"It's not a frat," Elliot said, closing the door behind me. "It's my cousin's place. His parents are out for a few days, so."

"Why are you bringing me here?" I said, leaving out, *as opposed to any other girl?*

He shrugged. "I don't know. Who are you, again?"

I blew out a laugh, rolling my eyes as we walked past the other cars toward the house. "Good one."

We headed around the side of the house, where the door was left ajar. Multicolored light poured out across the clean stoop and dark blades of grass. Elliot pushed the door aside, and we found ourselves in the midst of the rich and glam—twenty-somethings dripping Ralph Lauren bags and Balenciaga sneakers. Unlike the frat party, this place smelled of cologne more than weed, and all of the guests sipped from shot glasses and champagne flutes rather than plastic cups.

Elliot's natural habitat.

"In all seriousness, though," he continued, putting his hand on the small of my back, "you're here to seal your part of the deal."

I looked away from all the sparkle and bling, and up at him. "What do you mean?"

His hand moved from my shoulder up to my neck, then brushed my hair aside, combing his fingers through the purple strands. The petting was a favorite move of his.

"You didn't honestly think I would leave it at finger-fucking, did you?" he said, his voice so low we could've been speaking in front of a room full of high school teachers instead of drunk grad students.

Luckily, I didn't have to answer that. A young man burst through the crowd of people and embraced Elliot in a loose hug, clapping him on the back.

"Ell, man," he said, pulling back to display a similar sharp, dreamy grin, "thanks for coming! What's up? Who's this?"

I hadn't expected him to turn his attention on me so quickly, and I stuttered as I told him my name, introducing myself as, "an old classmate."

Elliot choked back a laugh at that statement. He tried to hide it, but I could tell, which was funny in of itself. We might have known each other for more than four years, but it only took a couple short car rides and a pit-stop at his dorm room to realize that maybe, just maybe, we had more in common than I'd ever thought we could.

It was the way he saw things—the way *we* saw things.

Or maybe I was just too much in my head. Yeah. Just because we had the same sense of humor for a split second didn't mean he'd changed.

I could never forget.

Never.

"Well, Kathleen," Elliot's cousin said, taking my hand in his and planting a playful kiss in my palm, "pleasure to meet you. Can I get you two drinks?"

Elliot nodded. "If you have rosé. Kat, anything?"

I shook my head. "I'm good, thanks."

His cousin left us, and we stood there, soaking in the chilled-out atmosphere. Despite being in a place I've never been to, amidst strangers, and standing beside a boy I'd considered a threat for pretty much my entire teenage life, I felt relaxed. More relaxed than I'd ever been. Maybe it was the deep lighting and the fur carpets, or the smell of expensive cigars.

Maybe.

"Rosé," Elliot's cousin said, returning as swiftly as he'd appeared. He handed a tall glass to me. "And water for the lady. Just because." He gave me a wink, and I accepted it with a half-smile.

"He's nice," I said, as he drifted back off into the crowd.

Elliot snorted and took a sip of his glass.

"A miracle we're related," he said, and let out an exaggerated gasp of satisfaction. He took my hand and started pulling me further into the house. "Upstairs."

"Yes, sir," I said, laughing as he ducked under a couple leaning in for a kiss in front of us, leaving me to swerve around them at last second.

"Smooth," he said, grabbing hold of me again as we walked up the wide spiral staircase. The marble surface of the steps clattered under my flats, and I watched the mass of beautiful people fall away from us as we ran up to the second floor. Never felt more like a fucking fairy princess.

"This is some ball," I joked as we stumbled past the last step. Before I could make another move, or even stop to look at our new surroundings, Elliot pushed me up against the wall. He kissed my neck.

"Oh my God," I said, pushing him away from me, smiling. "You weren't kidding."

"You thought I was?" he murmured, and dove back over me, sucking at the skin just beneath my ear, his hands moving from my shoulders down to my waist. I couldn't find the words to think, let alone speak.

I felt my body shift away from the wall as he started guiding me down the hall in slow, shuffling steps. I kept my eyes closed, let him hold me, take me. Everything he did—every kiss, every lick, seemed to say, *you're mine. All and only mine.*

"You," I managed to say, between gasping breaths, "had this all planned out, didn't you?"

Elliot chuckle, his breath tickling my skin. "More or less."

He guided me into a dimly lit room. Before I knew it, I was pressed between the soft caresses of a duvet and Elliot's arms as he touched me. I couldn't lie—this was a fantasy of four years in the making, all happening in a matter of minutes. I wanted to cry, it was so real.

But that's not who I was anymore.

"Wait," I gasped, surprised that he sat up, giving me room to breathe. Instead of pushing him off of me, I got up on my knees and shoved him onto the covers, climbing on top of him.

"Whoa," he said, blinking up at me. "Wasn't expecting you to go all dominatrix."

"That's a stretch."

Elliot smirked, relaxing under my hold. "Doesn't feel that way."

Rolling my eyes, I lifted my hands up his neck, feeling the skin under his dragon tattoo before cradling his face, sinking my hips deeper against his. His cock pressed up through the seat of his pants and up against my pussy and the sensation caused me to let out a slight gasp.

Before letting him go any further, I ground harder down against him, which elicited a sultry moan and a heavenly smirk from his lips. Elliot's cheeks blushed like fire, and on a whim, I pinched his cheek, just for the sake it.

"Let's make this quick," I muttered, shedding my top. "I have a thing to go to."

"Oh?" Elliot raised an amused eyebrow. "And what is that?"

I paused, and felt my own face flushing before replying, "A friend of mine. We're supposed to play board games, or something."

"God, you're cute," he said—his way of saying, *dork*—and sat up to plant a long, deep kiss on my lips.

Then, almost without parting from me, his lips fluttered across my jawline and down my neck as his hands moved up my back, undoing the rest of my shirt. I let him peel the shirt over my head until I sat bare. His touches felt almost caring, gentle, nothing like I'd imagined he would give me. If anything, the way I'd pushed him down on the bed, straddling him like a fucking wrestler was the most aggressive thing that'd happened so far between us. And it was my move, my call.

I wanted to keep it that way.

Pushing him back down onto the bed, I pressed my hips deeper against his and began rocking against him. I felt his cock grow harder under me, and I ground deeper into it, pressing my head down against his shoulder.

"Take em off," Elliot moaned, grabbing one of my wrists and guiding it to his waistline. "You're killing me, here."

Without saying anything, I began undoing his zipper as his hands glided over my back and undid my bra. Once his pants were undone, he kicked them off and tugged his shirt over his head all in two swift motions, as if he'd done this hundreds of times before—he *had* done this hundreds of times, I was sure of it.

"Hey," he whispered, once his chest was stark naked. I sat still atop him, watching as he eyed the straps of my bra before his eyes moved to mine. "What were you doing with Leo?"

I squinted at him. "What do you mean?"

"He picked up your phone when I called," he responded, raising an eyebrow as he moved a hand up my belly toward my bra.

"Yeah, I remember," I said. "Wasn't that part of your plan?"

His fingers paused as it made contact with the tight fabric.

"Plan?" He raised his other hand to begin slipping the straps off my shoulders. His touches sent shivers across my chest. "If that was part of the plan, he ruined it."

I shook my head, trying to hold in a gasp as he undid the clasp at my back. I felt the weight of an entire day's angst fall away from me as chilled air rushed over my breasts, hardening my nipples.

"Fuck," I whispered, more to myself than to Elliot. I couldn't believe I was doing this.

For a moment, my vision blurred, and I thought I might faint until Elliot sat up straight in front of me. As I remained sitting on his lap, he put his hands on my shoulders, looking into my eyes. My bra hung halfway over my breasts, the straps resting against the sides of my stomach. Despite my spastic heartbeats and the sweat that started beading at my neck, Elliot's eyes, those lush, green eyes, kept me cool enough.

"Why are you doing this?" I asked, forgetting to filter my words. But once they escaped, I didn't regret asking. It was a true question—a necessary one. "Why are you really doing this?"

His hands dropped from my shoulders, slowly, tenderly, and he rested them on the mattress behind him so that he still sat up, leaning back a little so that he gazed up rather than right at me.

And waited.

"You hate me," I continued, realizing that my voice was cracking. Tears bubbled up in my eyes faster than I wanted them to. "For the past four years, you've… hurt me."

My shoulders shuddered. The tears came out small, but the sniffles turned into chokes and sobs. Elliot stayed still. I dared not look him in the eyes out of fear that I might just see a stupid smirk, a cocked eyebrow, something to dismiss my years of humiliation and his years of inflicting that suffering.

Instead, I felt something soft against the base of my neck, and opened my bleary eyes. Elliot planted a soft trail of kisses along my collarbone, then down, slowly, in between my breasts. Everything seemed to go silent—a sweet silence—as my hiccupping sobs faded into deep breaths. I relaxed into his kisses like surrendering into the folds of a hammock, feeling like I was falling and being caught, over, and over again.

"You're right," he said finally, lifting his head so that his nose was inches from mine. "I'm an asshole."

I smiled, and before I knew what I was doing, I'd pushed him back onto the bed and kissed him.

Most of my life, I'd lived in my head. This was years of silence, or fantasy, of feelings, moving from my head and into reality. Into my life.

This was real.

This was my life.

And I was tired of being scared of living it.

I moved to the side of the bed for a split moment and took off my skirt. I stayed there beside him and watched as he reclined back onto the mattress, tucking his hands behind his head. Even though his body was skinny, he had a tight row of abs, and my stomach gave a flutter as his chest rose and fell as he breathed. Now it was only me, left in my panties, which were already soaked.

I couldn't believe it.

I just couldn't.

"You sure you're ready?" he asked, his eyes tracing the smudged lines of mascara around my eyes rather than looking into them.

Yes.

I've been ready for four years and you're overripe.

I climbed back on top of him so that my legs straddled either side of his, my pussy sitting right between his thighs. Slowly, I reached up to pull my bra up over my head, and tossed the cloth away from my body. For the first time, my chests were bare in front of another person, and it felt exhilarating.

I could do whatever I wanted to him and he didn't even know it.

Just like I'd done on that last day of school, I reached out to stretch the elastic of his boxers down to reveal his dick, pulsing with lust, hard, ready. Lowering myself over him, I started with a kiss on the side of his neck, down his tattoo. As I continued, I felt my nipples brush against his chest, and the tip of his cock rub against my belly button.

I could feel his hands skim over my shoulders and down my back. As I came closer to his own belly, my hand crept down his side and over his pelvis to fondle him while I kept the other stretched out, gripping his shoulder. As soon as my fingers touched his hot cock, he bucked beneath me. My panties grew wetter.

Yes.

I wanted this.

I wanted to fuck him. Hard.

Sinking further down his body, I moved my hands to his hips and lowered face closer and closer to his dick until my breath, hot despite my cold skin, rushed over the tip of his manhood and caused him to flinch.

"Do it," he seethed.

I lowered my lips to his cock, but instead of darting out my tongue to lick at the skin, I went all the way, and slipped the tip of his cock in my mouth. It felt hot, tasted slightly salty, and I couldn't help but giggle a bit as I dipped my head lower, taking more of him across my tongue, feeling his hips rise beneath me, sneaking more of himself past my lips.

I swirled my tongue around his cock as if it was my goal to feel every inch of him before he felt every inch inside me. Right now, he was mine, and I wanted to milk every second of it for what it was worth. I sunk my head a little deeper, and soon, established a slow, steady rhythm of sucking as he throbbed on top of my tongue.

Suddenly, I released him from my lips. Elliot gasped.

I sat back, wiping an arm across my mouth as a fat smirk spread across my lips. Turning onto my side, I slipped off my panties. They were drenched, already dousing our little corner of the room with the musty scent of sex.

Without giving him a second to protest, I climbed back on top of him in an almost downward-dog pose, supporting myself above him so that my breasts hung over his chest, my pussy was angled inches from his cock.

I could imagine it. Could already feel it plowing up, into me.

I'd fucking destroy him, I hated him so much.

"Whoa, wait." I hadn't noticed that Elliot had reached for his pants, which he'd discarded on the bed beside us, to pluck out a condom. He unwrapped it and had it rolled on within seconds. "Safety first."

"Shut up," I murmured, forcing my lips back to his.

Breaking away, I sucked in a sharp breath, and slowly, carefully, lowered myself onto him.

A tingling warmth rushed through my pussy as the tip of his shaft came in contact with my skin.

"You don't have to be on top," Elliot said, and I looked at his face to find him grinning like a maniac. He enjoyed seeing me struggle like this. Fucking sadist. "Wanna switch?"

"Don't be dramatic," I breathed.

Pushing my hips lower, I felt the head of his cock slip inside me. The sensation—slick heat—made my stomach go wild.

I lowered my forehead to his. His breath was warm against my lips, smelling faintly of alcohol. I didn't mind. Waiting a moment more, I took in a deep breath, then pushed my hips, slowly, lower onto him. His dick sunk up into me, and I felt him arch under my stomach, trying to press himself farther in.

I relented.

I felt a slight pinch of pain as my pussy expanded to accommodate his size. Taking in another sharp breath, I thrust my hips farther down, and flexed my legs wider on either side of him as his dick slid deeper inside. Realizing I'd been holding my breath, I dipped my head into Elliot's shoulder to let out a deep sigh.

"Still waiting for some action, sweetheart," Elliot whispered, turning his neck. As he spoke, I felt his teeth nibbling at my earlobe. It didn't do shit for me. He couldn't tell, but my hands were balling into fists at his sides.

He had a knack for getting me worked up about meaningless insults.

I thrust my hips down, taking him, all of him, inside me. The result was like lightening—dunking my head under the water in a hot bath without first dipping my toes in. The sensation ripped through me. My thighs trembled as I rose my hips once again, letting a little of him go, before plunging back onto him. The second time, his hips moved with me, and in moments, we were one, plunging, sculpting, fucking slow, fucking deep.

Soon, whatever twinges of pain that had sparked up in my pussy had dissipated, and I moved at a faster pace.

I slid him in and out of me, feeling my walls expand a little more with each thrust, each gasp of air.

"Fuck," I moaned. Elliot reached up his hand toward my backside as if to help guide me, encourage me. "I don't want to stop."

"Then don't," he hissed back, his fingers clenching around my ass cheek. He bucked his hips higher and higher as I rode him, and with one hand, I ran my fingers through his beautiful, jet black hair, buried my nose into it, loving the thick smell that now coated everything from his sweat to the tang of his shampoo.

We were moving fast now—up, down, up, down, in, out. I could feel my pussy growing numb with ecstasy, and a moment later, the surge of pleasure that could only be described as sultry—hungry, powerful, enough to pass me out across his chest—erupted through me.

"Not bad, Kitty Kat," Elliot breathed, his grip tightening on my shoulders as if he were afraid I'd fall to the floor as his own orgasm peaked within me. I still sat on top of him, his dick wedged all the way up in me. A smile streaked across my lips.

It was a wicked smile, and I didn't have to see it to know that. It was the smile of someone who'd won a majestic fucking battle—and I just did. I'd ridden the throne of high school agony, molded it into the shape that I wanted. Shame into glory.

And that's all I ever wanted.

Slowly, I lifted myself off of him, letting out a breath as his cock slid out of me. Both of us panting, I threw myself on the mattress beside him, and let us bask there in that moment for just a few seconds before pushing myself up to gather my clothes.

"What?" Elliot whined, sitting up. "That's it?"

I let out a snort. "What the fuck do you mean, *that's it?*"

He was stunned into silence. I didn't even think *he* knew what he meant. I'd gotten what I'd wanted—a shocked-stupid Vivian Russo—and he'd gotten what he'd wanted—pussy.

My part was done.

"Look," I said sarcastically, already pulling my shirt back over my bra, "I'd *love* to stay, but I got my own lame party to get to."

Now it was his turn to snort. "Lame is right."

Shrugging, I smoothed out my shirt, and moved to pull on my pants in a hurried motion as Elliot swung his legs over the side of the bed and reached for his own clothes. While I stared at him hard, unafraid, he kept stealing glances up at me as every inch of my skin that once had been forbidden to him was covered back up. I took my time, which must've killed him, and made me grin even more as I finally slipped on my shoes.

"See ya," I said, throwing up a peace sign as I sauntered out into the hallway, leaving him.

Once I knew I was out of his sight, checking over my shoulder to make sure he hadn't moved to watch me from the door, I ran down the hall and down the staircase, hiding my laughter with one hand as I held the railing with the other, and descended into the murmur of voices and music.

Must've been pure luck that Elliot's cousin's place happened to be so close to campus, because I was back in five minutes, striding through the drive way that led to the dorm building. A few late comers were walking out of the dining hall by the time I'd made it, and I picked up the pace, checking my phone to make sure that Tara hadn't gotten mad and decided to dis-invite me to her cute little get-together.

Nothing from her. She was either really chill, or too high to care.

Probably both.

Just as I reached for the door to enter to dorm lobby, I felt a hand on my arm, and got jolted back. Letting out a slight yelp, I spun around to find myself face to face with Leo.

That's all I knew before he forced his lips onto mine and pulled me back around the corner of the building and toward the ramp.

"Whoa," I yelled, breaking away from his hold at the top of the ramp. "What the hell are you doing?"

"What we were supposed to be doing before that douchebag interrupted us," he almost growled back, but regained his composure as he approached me once again, resting his hands on my shoulders. My first instinct had been to slap him, but my eyes found his—deep, icy blue, freezing me in his grasp.

"Interrupt what?" I said with a half-smile, half-grimace. "Giving you a hand-job?"

"What were you doing with him?" he asked at the same time I'd said hand-job—as if he wasn't expecting an answer, never wanted to hear one. In the first place. I stepped back from him, and his hands dropped reluctantly back to his sides.

"And you said he was the jealous one," I replied quietly.

He clenched his jaw.

"It's not that," he said, as if insulted by the idea of actually be attracted to me. "I was the one who pulled the stunt. *I* splashed hair dye all over your bitch of a roommate, not him."

"And?"

"So," he continued, sucking in a breath, "I should be the one who gets—"

"Rewarded?" I finished for him.

His eyes fell to the ground, and he stuffed his hands into his pockets, his posture crumpling. With that one word, I'd saved him from sounding that much more stupid, and I almost expected a "Thank you," if not, a nervous laugh. He gave neither.

"I was under the impression that it was Elliot who came up with the idea in the first place," I continued. "Is that true?"

He let out a sigh. "I guess."

"Then everything went according to plan," I said enigmatically, and reached out to give him a weak pat on the shoulder. "Gotta run."

With that, I turned and hurried back up the steps to the building and into the lobby, my heart feeling it was pulsing at the speed of Elliot's Mustang at eighty miles an hour. That was twice—*twice*—that I had either gotten, or almost gotten laid in a single day. I didn't think Pierre would've recognized the new me.

I didn't.

And I kind of liked that.

Once the elevator dropped me back off, I hurried over to Tara's room, finger-combing my hair back a bit before knocking so it wasn't *too* obvious I'd just gotten down and dirty with someone. Tara opened the door a second later, and the tinny smell of pot wafted out into the hall.

"Get in, quick," she giggled, giving me a little hug as she corralled me into the room. "Kenneth, meet my neighbor, Kat."

A smile flashed across my lips at the name, and I instantly recognized Kenny's face. Long hair, easy grin, blunt in his fingers. Same guy who'd convinced me to go confess my love to Eric the same day he'd decided it was Vivian he was fucking and not me.

"K and K," Tara giggled again, sounding more amused than she should've been. Result of the grass, no doubt. "Two K's. Ha!"

"We know each other," I laughed, sitting down on the floor beside him.

His eyes lit up, and he laughed. "Yo, how's it going? What happened with your friend?"

Tara looked eagerly between the two of us, waiting for the backstory. I decided I'd give it to them. Why the hell not?

I was in a good fucking mood.

"Remember when I met you for the first time?" I said, turning to face her.

She nodded. "Yeah. You were checking out my door."

"Well, I was heading to that ice cream social thing, and I met this guy there." I held up a finger before she could ask for a name. "I'll tell you one day. Anyway, I kind of liked him, or so I thought, and he was feeling me, too. But then Vivian, my roommate," I said, clarifying for Kenny, "brought me to that party at Powell. The dude was acting like a complete bitch, ignoring me, which was when I went outside and ran into, well, you."

Kenny nodded in approval. "And then we lived happily ever after."

"More or less," I snickered. "I was bawling my eyes out about the dude from the ice cream social—let's just call him Vinny—and he basically told me to follow my heart and go after him. Which I did—"

"And *then* it was happily ever after," Kenny interrupted. "Sorry. I mean, you're welcome."

"He was fucking my roommate," I said slowly, watching as Tara struggled to hold in her laughter. "Yeah. Plot twist."

"Oh, shit," Kenny coughed, setting down his blunt. "I'm sorry. Bad advice."

I shrugged. "It is what it is. I'm over it."

"But *he* isn't," Tara added, winking at me. I raised an eyebrow at her in return. "Come on," she laughed. "Vinny my *ass*. I heard you guys talking after you left my room. Don't know how you managed to rope in Eric Lamont, but it's obvious—he wants you *so* bad."

I narrowed my eyes at her. "You were eavesdropping, too?"

"Too?" Tara cocked her head to the side. "What do you mean?"

The fact that I'd just emerged from some haute cocktail party with my panties soaked through like a sponge crossed my mind, then the fact that I probably didn't want to explain how or why I'd gotten to that point in the first place.

"Never mind," I said, waving it off. "You know Eric?"

"Hell yeah, I do," Tara giggled, her voice reaching her highest possible pitch. I had to admit, getting used to her on weed was going to take some time. "I used to have a *fat* crush on him in high school."

"Oh, really?" I said. "Isn't that funny?"

Despite her love for pot and my affinity for dark color schemes, the similarities between us didn't seem to end.

"Let me guess," I continued, leaning toward her, resting my chin in the cup of my palm. "He was popular, you weren't, and he just so happened to brush past you in the hall one day with that look in his eye."

"How romantic," Kenny monotoned. "Can we play *Sorry!*, now?"

"Close," Tara said, ignoring her friend. "He was a semi-nice jock I'd just so happened to be put in a summer camp with."

"Semi," I repeated, shaking my head at her. "Right. I forgot, he's a Jersey boy."

"And I'm a Cali girl," she said, and that shy smile I'd come to know so well on her resurfaced, just for a moment. "Something tells me you don't really care about him."

I let out a snort. "I care about him as long as his affection for me keeps Vivian foaming at the mouth."

"Hm." Tara sat back against her bed, and let out a long, thoughtful breath. Smoke curled up around her head like a halo. "I see."

Something I'd said must've set off the mood, because her smile drooped a bit at the corners. Kenny glanced from me to her, as if he expected me to be the one to break the silence. Squinting at Tara, I tried to read the expression in her gaze. If the human body had a lie detector, it'd be in the eyes.

Then it clicked.

"You don't..." I began, piecing it together as I spoke, "still like him, do you?"

Tara lowered her blunt, resting her wrist across her knees as she drew them up to her chest. "Maybe."

I smiled at her. "I don't like him, you know. Seriously."

"Don't be serious," she said, reciprocating the smile. "Nothing about this is serious. Even if your roommate wasn't trying to get her hands all over him, I doubt he'd ever like me back."

"You kidding?" I grabbed onto her legs, scooting myself closer to her. "If he's going after someone like *me*, you one hundred percent have a chance of being with him."

She looked me up and down, the same way Vivian had done just days before. Instead of casting a condescending look back in response, she put her hand on mine.

"Thanks," she laughed. "I'll try to take that as a compliment."

Kenny had been drumming his fingers on the top of the *Sorry!* box for the past five minutes, and the second I glanced back at him with a guilty smile, he threw the lid onto the floor.

"Done?" he said, already unfolding the board.
"Good. We're playing."

"Fine." Tara snatched the blue piece from the puddle of cards he'd thrown in the center of the board. She handed the piece to me. "Kat goes first."

"Hey," I said, impressed, "that's my favorite color."

"Why does she get to go first?" Kenny whined.

Tara handed him the red piece. "Because she's the guest."

"*What?*" Kenny screeched, throwing his hands in the air. I collapsed back against Tara's bed in laughter. "She practically *lives* here."

"And?" Tara smirked.

Once everything was arranged, I picked up a card, and my pieces ended up remaining in my little bubble of my side of the board. Tara went next, and one of her pieces escaped onto the perimeter of the board. Kenny's pieces, like mine, were undisturbed.

"So," I said, reaching for another card, "how do you guys know each other, anyway?" I looked at Kenny. "You're from Powell, right?"

"*No,*" he said, dragging out the word as if the thought were an abomination. "The only reason I was at that frat house was because I got lost on my way to a basement party."

I snickered. "Sure."

"In all honesty," he exclaimed. "Maybe it was the weed."

"Yeah," Tara replied, rolling her eyes. "How about next time, you *don't* smoke while riding your bike into unfamiliar territory?"

One of my pieces was finally ahead on the board by about two spaces, a big accomplishment in of itself, considering Kenny's was still locked into place and Tara's had to be moved back a space. As Kenny was contemplating his next move, which was between moving one piece forward altogether or splitting his advance, Tara reached for her phone and plugged it into her portable speaker.

"You like Billie Holiday, right?" she asked, grinning at me.

I nodded. "Great idea."

As the sweet jazz began to float through the speaker, Tara stood up to crack open a window. "Should'a done that before," she said, putting a finger to her mouth. "Oopsie."

"Anyway," Kenny continued, "while that ice cream thing was going on, I met this gal while she was sitting under a tree reading a book on the quad, like the shy girl of my dreams. So, naturally, I *had* to go up to her."

"You're full of it, Kenneth," Tara snickered.

"I see," I said, smiling at the two of them. I had to agree with Kenny on this one—they *were* cute together. Acted as if they've known each other for years instead of days, just like best friends.

She was too good for someone like Eric.

The night continued on as it was, talking about love and high school, cracking stupid jokes about setting off the fire alarm. Three hours rolled by, then four, then five. Tara fell asleep in Kenny's arms as we forgot about the game, and I spread a blanket over the two of them, blowing them each a kiss before slipping out into the hallway.

They were too adorable.

Most of all, I was just relieved that Tara hadn't asked too many questions about Leo, where I'd gone with him, and why I hadn't made it to her room until an hour had gone by.

If she had, I didn't know what I would've said.

My room was only a few doors down from Tara's, but as soon as I closed her door behind me, I could hear the throbbing of music and shrieks of laughter coming from my room. Seemed like the Queen Bee made some new friends. As I crept closer, it looked like the door was cracked open just wide enough for the noise to be *too* obnoxious.

I swallowed and turned to look back at Tara's door before facing mine again.

No way I was going in there.

Eyeing the empty lounge, spending the night on the couch seemed pretty tempting—until I heard something.

"Oh my God," said some unnaturally high-pitched voice, "this girl's getting more action than she's allowed to."

"Ugly bitch," said another.

"Ugly hoe is more like it."

It was hard to hear anything more with the music blaring from within, and I was surprised an RA hadn't come barreling down the hall to scold them for it yet. Pressing my back against the wall by the doorframe, I waited for another moment, trying to find the courage to go into my own room.

But I didn't have to.

"Well, well, if it isn't our favorite person," Vivian squeaked, poking her head out the door. Her lips spread in a wicked, red-lipstick grin to match her red-streaked hair. "We were just talking about you."

"Oh, yeah?" I said flatly. "More like shitting on me."

She let out a little snicker, as if in agreement. Another girl, someone I hadn't met before, stuck her head out beside her and gave me a once-over. Vivian looked back at her, and they giggled as they dipped back into the room.

"Fuck my life," I muttered under my breath, and took in a long breath before pushing the door aside.

It seemed as if Luna, the new girl, and Vivian had formed a little pow-wow in the center of the room, a string of fairy lights and wine bottles decorating the floor as the three of them sat in a circle, their three phones on the carpet, glowing like a blue fire between them. Keeping my eyes up, I stepped around them to reach my side of the room.

"Hey, so…" I said, turning around to find that they were paying zero attention to me. I cleared my throat. "Hey, I need to go to bed."

They still didn't seem to hear me. Or they were just being inconsiderate.

Definitely the latter.

"Can your friends head out? I need to get ready for bed," I said, raising my voice as I looked at Vivian. She made eye contact with me, but looked away as she covered her mouth, smirking. "It's, like, three in the morning."

Vivian looked to her friends, then back at me. With a sigh, she stood up once again, turning off the music from her phone. For some weird reason, the sudden quiet felt more intimidating than staring into her eyes did.

"Fine," she said flippantly, as if the whole idea of her friends evacuating our own room was negotiable. "You're right. It is pretty late. In fact, I was about to text your mom to inform her about you going past curfew."

I practically spat out my next breath. "What? *Curfew?*"

Vivian raised her eyebrows, nodding like it wasn't the most untrue thing in the world. We both knew full well that we didn't have a curfew at Freeman. I moved to reach for her phone, but she held it back.

"Why do you have my mom's number?" I asked slowly, narrowing my eyes at her. "And why would you text her *anything?*"

Dipping her head to the side, she gave me a hurt look.

"Don't you remember?" she said, drawing her eyebrows together in exaggerated concern. "You asked me to take it down, just in case anything happened to you. Like, I don't know, getting into a stranger's car and not coming home until three in the morning."

I just stared at her.

Anger boiled within me, but I was confused more than anything.

"What?" I whispered. "You saw me get into someone's car?"

Elliot's car.

Still keeping that stupid, fake expression of concern pasted to her face, Vivian swiped through her phone, and shoved it in my face. A short video clip played, angled from our window, looking down at me as I crossed the sidewalk and slipped into Elliot's black Mustang.

Shaking my head, I pushed the phone away.

"That could be anyone's car," I said. "Not some stranger's. I *know* the guy."

"Hm." Vivian raised her eyebrows, looking back down at her phone. A smirk played on her lips. "Apparently, so does your *mother*. And she's not happy about it."

What was she talking about?

I pulled out my phone and froze. There were ten missed calls, a dozen texts—all from my mom.

"Oh my God," I murmured, turning away from Vivian as her two sidekicks began giggling. "Shit. Shit. Shit. *Shit*."

My mom might not have known about how Elliot and his gang had treated me the past four years, but she sure as hell knew who they were—if anyone, she knew who Elliot was, and his family. *Everyone* in our town did. If it was any other prick bullying me, I would've brought it up to her in a heartbeat.

But with him, things were... complicated.

"Anyway," Vivian sighed, "your mom didn't seem to like the fact that you just got into a car owned by her *ex.*" She put a hand to her mouth, just as Tara had done, as if also to say, *Oopsie.* "Sorry, ex-*husband.*"

The air left my lungs. Stepping back, putting my hand against the door handle.

"What do you mean?" I breathed, heat crawling up to my temples. "What are you talking about?"

I backed myself up against the door, feeling my knees buckle under me. My head was starting to spin. I could only hear her voice—that stupid, shrill voice—echoing around me.

Husband.

Ex-husband.

"Oh, yes," Vivian said. "According to her, he was, and I quote, 'an emotionally abusive wreck who cheated and stole thousands from my savings.'"

She looked up at me as if she'd just finished reading a passage in a textbook, as if she didn't see the tears welling in my eyes.

"She…" I gulped, "my mom said that to you?"

Nodding, Vivian pressed her lips into a pitying grin. "Apparently, you're not the only one in your family who has issues."

"What the *fuck* are you talking about?" I shrieked, lunging for her phone. She simply stepped aside. I collapsed against her desk, already dizzy to begin with. This felt all too familiar. "How dare you talk about my mom like that," I muttered, glaring at her. "Why do you even care?"

She simply shrugged. Not even a hint of remorse.

I couldn't take it anymore.

Gritting my teeth, I forced myself back upright, pulled the door open, and dashed back out into the hallway, letting the door slam closed behind me. I sunk down against the wall and buried my face into my knees. Hot tears streamed down my cheeks.

None of this made sense.

Ex-husband?

My mom never talked about anyone besides my dad. He may have been skeevy, but he was anything but a bloodthirsty Lancaster.

Taking in a deep breath, I looked at my phone, and found my mom's contact. My finger hovered over her number for a few long seconds before I pressed down on it and brought the phone to my ear.

She picked up immediately.

"Hey," I whispered, pushing myself up to my feet. "Mom, I—"

"You're coming home."

Her voice was cold. Colder than it'd ever been before. I could tell she was trying not to raise her voice, not to shriek into the phone. I didn't know what to say. I was confused. I didn't know how much she knew, how much Vivian knew, and how much she'd told.

"Mom," I whispered, beginning to pace down the hall. "What's going on?"

As soon as I was starting to enjoy myself for once, as soon as I was just beginning to fit in, drama had to ensue. No—this wasn't drama. This was my mom, and my family. It wasn't just about me. Not anymore.

Which made things ten times harder.

I heard a deep sigh from the other end of the line, then a few seconds of silence before she spoke again.

"You know Elliot," she said, as if it wasn't a question. It wasn't. "You went to school with him, correct?"

I echoed her sigh. "Yeah."

"Then you know about his family, what they're like," she replied carefully, a little calmer. I knew this couldn't be easy for her. "Look. Before I became involved with your father, I'd already been, well… married to Frank Lancaster."

Fuck.

I saw where this was going.

"By *involved*, you mean…" I took in a trembling breath. "You cheated. On *him*. On… Frank."

On Elliot's dad.

I couldn't breathe.

"Yes," she whispered, sounding so tired, so defeated. "Look, honey, I'm sorry I didn't tell you all this before, it's just… I didn't know you were close to his son. It just makes things more—"

"Complicated?" I snapped, and bit down on my tongue.

I couldn't help it. The confusion, the angst, was turning to pure, boiling rage. Now, everything made sense. And the truth hurt.

I still didn't know how much she really knew. If anything, my mom only knew what Vivian had told her, which was that I'd gotten in a car with her ex's son and didn't come back until hours later. Of course, my bitch-ass roommate didn't have the whole story—she didn't know that I'd spent the majority of that time hanging out in Tara's room, not with Elliot.

But it didn't matter.

"There's a lot of history between us," my mom continued. "I didn't know that his son was going to school so close to you. I just think… it would be better if you transferred."

My breath hitched in my throat. Now, the tears didn't bother me. I was truly frozen. Stuck. I felt nothing.

Numb.

"Why?" I breathed. "That… doesn't make sense. I went to school with the kid for four years."

"I know, honey, I know, it's just—" I waited her to finish, and could've sworn I heard a sniffle before she continued, "when you were in school, you weren't involved with this boy. You had friends at Woodman. I didn't want to uproot your whole life there just because of something that I'd done."

I snorted.

"Mom," I muttered, "I don't think you know as much about my life at Woodman as you think you do."

"Well, instead of holing up everything inside, maybe you could've *told* me."

We became silent, and it was torture. She was right. I could've been more open, could've been more honest. But she didn't want to know. She didn't want to know about being laughed at every day, teased, groped, tripped. I didn't *want* her to know.

It would've been too much.

"Anyway," she said, testing the waters once again, "you've worked too hard in high school to be put into a situation where, well, you might become a target. Classes haven't started. If you transferred, you could take the semester off and start again in the spring somewhere else. That's all I'm saying."

I had to press a hand against my mouth to keep from spitting out in laughter. *A target.* I was already a target. Been one from the start.

Right.

Vivian.

I lowered the phone from my ear as the thoughts came crashing together.

If I left, that meant Vivian would win. This was what she wanted—me, gone. Out of her period blood-red hair. Somehow, she was smart enough to mess up my life by doing so from the inside-out. If I agreed to transfer, she'd succeed.

I couldn't let her.

I had to hold my ground.

"Mom, I'm sorry, but," I said slowly, lifting the phone back up to my lips, "you don't need to worry about me. If something happens between me and Elliot, I can deal with it. On my own. I promise."

I lowered the phone and hung up. Leaning back against the wall, my mind went blank. There was only one feeling—a cold, slick sensation, like shadows, clouding my thoughts, like the gathering of a storm. Anger. Hatred. Confusion.

Clamping my jaw tight, I lifted my phone back up and searched for Elliot's Instagram.

I didn't care so much that my mom didn't tell me about her affair with my dad, or even the fact that she'd been married to Frank Lancaster. But I couldn't ignore that the reason Elliot had been bullying me all these years just because…

No. I couldn't make assumptions.

I'd just have to find out, once and for all.

Hey, I texted. *We need to talk.*

I waited for a minute. Two. Paced up and down the hall a couple of times before opening his DMs again. *Elliot,* I wrote. *Where are you right now?* Another few minutes. No response.

I couldn't blame him. It *was* past three in the morning.

Letting out a long, heavy sigh, I looked back to my room. The music had started up again. Didn't look like Vivian and her cronies were going to leave any time soon. Even if they were, I wasn't in the mood for sleep. I *couldn't* go to sleep—not after finding out that the root of all my years of torture was not because of some fault of my own.

It was my mom's. She cheated on Elliot's dad. And now, he probably hated her guts—and mine. No shit.

But these were just theories. I had to get more information from the source of all this angst. I'd go to Powell. I'd find Elliot. And settle this.

Vivian might've found a way to get under my skin and practically boot me out of college with nothing more than a stupid video clip and a text to my mom, but even she would have to follow through.

Elliot and I still had scheming to do.

6

Maybe jogging the thirty blocks to Powell alone at four in the morning in full-on rain wasn't the *smartest* thing to do, but hey—I'd just lost my virginity, played a three-hour long game of *Sorry!* and found out that my mom used to fuck my high school bully's dad. All in one night.

I had to cut myself some slack.

By the time I arrived at Powell's front gates, I'd gotten a couple massive pit-stains and could drink ten gallons of anything, but I'd done it. I'd made it. And I wasn't going to quit now.

"Elliot, here I come," I breathed, dragging myself through the front doors of his dorm building like a wet cat, flashing the back of my Freeman ID. The kid behind the desk didn't even notice the move, or didn't care. "You fucking douchebag."

Breezing in past the front desk to the elevator, and up to Elliot's floor was all a blur, and as I stepped out into the hall, the sound of my own heart beating against my chest blotted out everything else.

My head was blank. My heart was not.

It was raging.

I strode up to Elliot's door, panting, and rapped my knuckles on the wood. Stepping back, I shoved my hands in my pockets, and waited a few moments before yanking out my phone. Still no response. Radio silence.

Forcing in a deep breath, I knocked again. Hard.

A second later, I heard something crash and fall within the room, then a curse. Slippers shuffling across the carpet.

The door opened.

"What the *fuck*—" Felix stood there, staring back at me. "Oh."

"Where's Elliot?"

Felix reached up to rub his eyes, muttering another curse under his breath just as Leo came shuffling over to the door to peer over his shoulder. Recognizing me, he smiled. I didn't.

"Look," Felix said, and sucked in a long breath. "He's not here."

I raised an eyebrow. Didn't believe a word he just said.

"Oh, yeah?" I said, already trying to pry my way past him. "Let me see."

"Whoa, what's going on?" Leo said, jumping back as I pushed past the two of them. "Why's she here?"

"She kinda has a right to be here," I heard Felix murmur just as I finished scanning the bunk beds to find that he was right. No Elliot.

I turned back to face him.

"What do you mean?" I said, lowering my voice to match his. Through the shadows, Felix's dark eyes still pierced mine. "And where's Elliot?"

Felix turned to Leo and shared a look. Their eyes seemed to have a whole conversation in that span of two seconds, a technique perfected from years of hanging out, no doubt, before he turned back to me.

"Come with me," Felix said, moving back into the room to grab his phone. With a shrug, Leo headed back to his bed, flopping down onto the mattress.

Felix went back into the hall, and I followed him, his words churning in my head as he shut the door quietly behind us.

I had a right to be here.

Did he know about me and Elliot? Our *parents*?

"Let's go in the lounge," Felix said, already a yard ahead of me, swaying down the hall like he'd been drugged. Sleep counts for something, I guess.

He pushed open the glass door, and the motion-sensing lights automatically flickered on. The place was nice. A full kitchen, a couple sofas, a bean bag, and a flat screen TV. Felix plopped himself down into the bean bag, and I sat on the sofa, crossing my legs tensely.

"So?" I said, keeping my expression neutral. I became very aware of the sweat that had tracked itself across my forehead on my way here, and I eyed the sink. "Wait a sec."

I got back to my feet and went over to the sink, turning on the faucet to splash some water on my face. I didn't care what Felix thought as I went rifling through a couple of the cabinets to find a stack of plastic cups, taking one to fill. I gulped the whole twelve ounces of ice-cold water in less than ten seconds.

"Fuck," I sighed. "That's better."

"We do have a water fountain, you know," Felix replied. "Like, down the hall."

"Right, thanks," I said, setting the cup down onto the counter. "Because I'd rather stick my face into some metal petri dish."

Felix snorted at the comment.

"God," he said, slumping back in the bean bag, dragging his hands down his face. "It's too late for this shit."

"Then let's get this over with," I said, returning to the couch. "Where is he? Where's Elliot?"

"How about we start from, let's see, the *beginning*," Felix said, motioning with his hands up, then down. "Because, like, we'll get to the good stuff, but first, I was just wondering—"

"Shut up," I said. "You know more than you act like you do."

He smirked at that remark. I'd use it as leverage. Felix was right, after all. If he was giving me the time of day, I might as well start from the beginning. It's not like Elliot was here, anyway.

"Why *is* Elliot going to school here?" I began, leaning forward to rest my chin in my hands. "In fact, why are all of you going to school here? Aren't you all, how do I put this lightly..." I tapped my chin sarcastically, as if searching for the phrase Pierre and I had already perfectly curated for the past four years. "... trust fund babies?"

"Wow. Harsh." Felix cracked another smirk. "Elliot's family is broke."

I narrowed my eyes at him. When he didn't elaborate, I'd assumed the joke was nonexistent.

"Elliot's dad declared bankruptcy at the beginning of senior year," he continued, his smile slipping. "So, yeah. Plot twist. He's poor."

I shook my head, still processing his words.

"What?" I whispered. "How?"

Felix shrugged.

"Didn't say. Doesn't really matter to me, to be honest. I don't ask questions. Leo and I... between the two of us, we've been carrying his family for the past few months. Elliot's been staying at my house since January." He paused, noticing the expression twisting on my face. He took in a deep breath. "So, yeah. Going to a school out of state wasn't an option for him, but he was adamant about moving out of his parents' place. With all the shit going on between them, it made complete sense. So, here we are. Three roommates, splitting rent at a third-rate public university a ten-minute drive away from our hometown."

He shrugged, a tired laugh escaping his lips. When he looked back up at me to find that I wasn't amused, he dropped the look.

"Not that there's anything wrong with a place like Powell," he said slowly. "Or Freeman."

"I accept your apology," I said, rolling my eyes. "*Now* can you tell me where he is?"

Felix opened his mouth as if about to reply, but then quickly closed it. I wasn't about to let that slip.

"Hey, don't censor yourself now, pretty boy," I said. "It's a simple question."

"It's really not," he responded, suddenly sitting upright. "Now that your airhead roommate got wind of all this shit happening between you and Elliot—and that your *mom's* involved—it kinda adds a whole other layer of confusion to this thing."

"Wait, just wait," I said, putting my hands to my temples. "How do *you* know that my mom's in on this?"

"Your roommate sent the video to your mom, right?"

I nodded.

"Well, your mom must've sent it to Elliot's dad, or told him about it, because Elliot found out and told *me*," Felix answered.

"I don't get it. All Vivian did was send a video to my mom of me getting into Elliot's car," I said. "I get why my mom found it weird, but why does anyone else care?"

"It wasn't just *that* video," Felix sighed, and pulled out his phone. "Look, I don't know how else to break this to you, but…"

He extended his phone over to me. After a moment's hesitation, I took it, swallowing as I looked down at the screen.

I threw it right back at him.

"What the *hell*?" I said, standing up. "What the hell *is* that?"

It was a rhetorical question. I knew exactly what the fuck that was. A video. Of me. And him.

Fucking.

"Why the hell would you show me that?" I hissed, trying to hold back from screaming, from kicking the coffee table to its side. "How? How did she—"

"You wouldn't believe me if I didn't show you!" Felix fired back, pushing himself off the bean bag and onto his knees. Grabbing my hair in my hands, I began pacing around the room.

The party. Of course. Elliot's cousin's house.

We'd gone upstairs, where we'd thought no one would be. Just like she had done with Eric the night before that.

And what had I done?

Right.

I'd spied on them. I'd watched them fuck on a bed that wasn't their own, in a house that wasn't their own, in a way that was so scandalous that it could've been a parody of every angsty coming-of-age romcom ever created. House party and sex. Jealousy. I was there, watching all of it. Hearing all of it.

Maybe, as she'd been lying there, looking past Eric's shoulders, she'd seen me squatting at the door, looking through the crack. And maybe doing the same to me was her way of getting back. Touché.

The only difference?

I hadn't been *filming* the whole fucking thing.

"Let me guess," I muttered, settling back down onto the couch a few deep breaths later. "She also sent it to the university president under my school email as an attempt to get me expelled."

Jealousy. I was coming to see what it could do to a person.

Fuck Eric.

"Not exactly." Felix drew in a shaky breath. "I'm assuming you haven't heard the news."

I let out an exasperated huff of air. "*What* news? Why are you being so cryptic?"

Felix bent over his knees, running his hands nervously for his hair. "Fuck," I heard him mutter under his breath. "Fuck, fuck, fuck."

"What?" I almost shrieked, pushing myself off of the couch to go stand over him. "What's going on? What *else* could she possibly do?"

I could feel the tears burn through my eyelids as he looked up at me.

"I'm sorry," he whispered, holding up his phone. "I'm just… so sorry, Kat."

I snatched it away from him, my heart beating so fast I wouldn't be surprised if it was a ticking time bomb ready to explode, send my thoughts and feelings flying in all directions. I squinted down at the screen, struggling to keep my breaths somewhat steady. It was a link to *The News & Observer*, Raleigh's newspaper. It was a short news story about a local boy who had attempted suicide while overseas studying.

It was about Pierre.

I dropped the phone to the floor.

"I'm sorry," Felix said again, standing up and reaching out as if to catch me. "I'm really—"

"What the fuck," I hissed, slapping away his arm. "Is this some kind of cruel joke?"

I couldn't breathe.

I couldn't breathe.

I couldn't.

"Don't understand," I whispered, my voice shaking a hundred times more than my hands as I bent down to claw Felix's phone from the floor. Holding my breath, I scanned the screen again, looking more closely at the details.

I couldn't believe it.

My Pierre.

He attempted suicide.

"Why?"

The word came out so meek. Almost silent, because I refused to believe it.

"What…" I shut my eyes tight. "What does this have to do with Vivian, or my mom, or *anything*?"

Not that it mattered.

Not that anything mattered anymore.

Slowly, I lowered myself back to the couch, and let the sobs rush over me. Tears came flooding over my cheeks, burning my skin like acid, and even though I gasped and heaved and tried, so hard, to grasp at the air, I still couldn't breathe.

I couldn't believe it.

Pierre.

Felix watched me for a few moments, allowing me the time to drown myself in my confusion and agony, before getting up from the beanbag and coming over to sit beside me. As he laid an arm over my shoulders, I realized just how cold I'd been—just how much the rain had already done and what my snot and tears were doing to me now.

Suffocate me.

"She sent the video to him," Felix explained, slowly. His warmth radiated from his voice just as much as it did from his body as he pulled me closer. He was trying his best to tread carefully. "I think… he liked you. More than you know."

Suddenly, I choked. And looked at him.

"Why the fuck," I seethed, "would you, of *all* people, know anything about my friend?"

I elbowed his arm off my shoulder and turned to face him completely.

"You fucking asshole." My voice was way past a whisper, now. Way past a scream, it was so small. "All of you. Elliot. Leo. You spend four years treating us like shit, and now, you think you know us?"

Felix didn't seem to object. He waited, eyes nodding while he kept still, listening.

He knew I wasn't going to end there.

"If Pierre really liked me," I continued, stumbling across the words like they were in a dream, and my mind was full of static, "he wouldn't try kill himself because he saw me fucking someone else. He saw me fucking one of *you*. Fucking *Elliot*."

Leaning over my knees, I buried my face in my hands.

What have I done?

How could I?

How?

"I wouldn't have done it if it weren't for her."

I said the words before they even registered in my brain. They came from the heart. Straight from the source of angst herself.

I lifted my head, my thoughts spiraling into a storm cloud. A hurricane.

"If it weren't for Vivian," I murmured, "this would never have happened."

Turning back to face Felix, it felt as if it'd been days since I'd actually looked him in the eye. For some reason, my vision seemed clearer with tears blotting out everything else around it.

Maybe it was the hatred. The anger.

Adrenaline.

"We have to get back at her," I said, my voice coming out stronger. "*I* have to. For Pierre."

For my own sanity.

Once again, Felix let his eyes do all the talking. I didn't have to see his lips move to know that he was in. Whatever his true motives were, I didn't care. He *was* here, wasn't he?

Something, anything about this, must've mattered to him.

"Where is Elliot?" I tried again. This time, answering wasn't negotiable. If he didn't cut to the chase within two seconds, I'd clamp my hands around his neck. "Where. Is. He?"

"His dad pulled him out of school," he responded, seeming to catch my drift. "At least, just for a little while. Until all this drama calms the fuck down."

I let out a snort. Drama.

This wasn't drama.

This was avenging my friend.

"Well, can he come here?" I said. "Or do we have to haul ass all the way back to our hometown?"

Felix smirked. And I could tell that it was going to be the latter.

"You up for a little road trip?" he said, standing up from the couch. Instead of heading right back toward the door, he offered me his hand. And smiled. "Not that fifteen minutes is much of a trip, but you know what I mean."

I raised an eyebrow in suspicion at his outstretched hand. I moved to take it, but at the last moment, even as our fingertips brushed, I pulled back.

"I don't care, you know," I said, the thought occurring to me as the words spilled from my lips. But I just had to say it. "About Elliot being poor. Couldn't give a crap. Makes sense that he'd want to go to a cheaper school, but still…"

Felix bit his lip, as if he knew where this was going.

"So?" I pressed, and couldn't help the smirk spreading on my own lips. "Why'd he choose Powell? Over any other public college in the area?"

Felix shrugged.

"Maybe it was a matter of being close, but just far enough," he replied, wiggling his perfectly groomed eyebrows at me. "Make what you will of that."

I shook my head at him and took his hand. "Whatever."

Felix lifted me up to my feet, and after taking a moment to draw in a deep breath and wipe the tears from my eyes, I followed him out of the lounge and back into the hallway. Instead of turning left like I thought he would to head to the elevator, he turned back in the direction of his room.

"Can't leave Leo behind," he explained, whispering over his shoulder. Funny that Felix, one of the most party-hard-and-loud people I knew, would have any consideration for those living around him.

"Whatever," I said again, crossing my arms. "Just hurry up."

He obeyed. Less than ten seconds later, Felix returned, Leo sauntering close behind in a beanie and flip-flops. Unlike Felix, he seemed to have a little less awareness for the passed-out drunk and sleeping kids in the rooms around us as his feet squeaked across the floor in the dead silence.

Even though fury had shoved aside the sadness and guilt that had rushed through me just minutes ago, Pierre's face still flickered in and out of my vision. I had to keep my chin high and force myself to breathe to keep myself from letting any more teardrops streak my face.

Once we'd squeezed into the elevator, I took the moment to check my phone, to scroll back through our text messages, look over any missed calls from Pierre. There was nothing.

Well, shit.

That was a lie.

There was one missed call from a few hours ago. No, way more than a few. It had to be around the time that Elliot had whisked me away to that stupid party at his cousin's place.

How hadn't I seen it?

I swiped to Pierre's number and pressed call. There was a moment of silence before his voice echoed in my ear, but it was just his voicemail. I hung up and tried again. The same message greeted me again. I went to my phone's dialer to try the hospital when I realized I had no idea where he had been taken. With no other options, I flipped to my text messages and sent:

Pierre, call me as soon as you see this. Please.

Frustrated, I shoved my phone into my pocket and tightened my jaw again. I wanted to punch myself in the face. Trap myself in a dark room and never come out. Starve.

This wasn't fair to Pierre.

He didn't deserve this.

Who did?

"So, let me guess," I said, looking at Felix as we stepped out of the elevator, "Elliot's wallowing in some dark and dingy corner of your mansion?"

"Not exactly," he said. "His dad found a small apartment to rent in our neighborhood. He's staying there."

I stopped in my tracks.

"Wait," I said, looking between him and Leo. "I did *not* sign up to meet Frank Lancaster."

"You won't have to," Leo said, a warm smile flashing across his lips. He put an arm around me and started walking again. "We'll lure Elliot out for you, don't worry."

"You better."

Even though we were returning home, after all this, I wasn't ready to see my *own* mom, let alone the dude who hated my guts because of her. If it came down to it, and I had to talk to him, it all came back to Pierre. At this point, I wouldn't shy away from anything if it meant doing something, anything, for him.

How could I have been so selfish?

We made it through the lobby and out onto the sidewalk, early sunlight lining roofs of the campus the buildings. A new day. A new start. Last night, something had almost ended. Someone.

It didn't have to be that way.

I was going to deal with the consequences, no matter what. For the both of us.

We made it into the parking garage, and into Felix's car before I even knew it. If I had to guess, the car couldn't have been more than a few weeks out of the shop, still reeking of that new car scent that almost made me want to hold my nose. Wouldn't be surprised if his daddy had bought it for him just for college.

I took the back seat, and Leo the front. Felix started the engine, and we rolled out in silence, deep in our own thoughts.

"Pierre," I whispered, a whisper so small that even I couldn't hear it. Just mouthing the words. "I'm sorry."

There was nothing else to say.

Actions, of course, spoke louder than words. And with my actions, I'd make it up to him. I'd make everything, everything, up to him.

Vivian was going down.

I couldn't have it any other way.

7

Felix ended up going fifty in a twenty mile per hour zone, which was fine by me. We crept up against the curb in front of Elliot's new apartment building in less than ten minutes. As I left the car, I could feel my pulse rising, as if I'd just stepped out of a rocket ship and onto the moon.

Thrill.

And fear.

"Okay," I breathed, looking up at the mass of gray brick that made up the apartment complex. "You guys go in, and I'll wait out here."

"Uh-uh. No way you're standing out here alone," Leo said, looping his arm back over my shoulder until I shoved it off. Just because I almost gave him a hand job didn't mean he could get closer to me in any other way. "Sorry. I'll stay here with you, Felix will go."

"Whatever," Felix said, already walking off toward the entrance, tossing and catching his keys in his hand.

We watched him go into the building. As soon as he disappeared, I leaned back against the car, crossing my arms. My mind could only focus on one thing, one face, one name. And as much as I bit down on my tongue to feel some other type of pain, nothing could make Pierre's voice go away. The voice I should've heard at the other end of the line when he'd called. The call I'd missed.

Was this all my fault?

Was it even real?

"Hey," Leo said, breaking the tense silence between us as he slipped his hands into his front pockets and joined me against the side of the car. "I'm sorry about your friend."

"Sure you are."

Even though I didn't turn to look at him, I could feel his gaze sharpen on me.

"What the fuck is your problem?"

Now I looked at him, barely resisting the urge to slap him across the face.

"What's *my* problem?"

"Yeah." Leo glared at me. For a moment, all I saw was Pierre's eyes, seething. "I'm just trying to be sympathetic."

I let out a harsh laugh, facing the building again. I didn't want to look at him. Scumbag.

"You bullied us for four fucking years in a row," I muttered. "Nothing can make me believe your sympathy."

We fell into another bout of uncomfortable silence, which said more about our feelings than either of us probably cared to admit. He knew I was right. Yet, for some reason, he was here, standing beside me. All three of them—despite everything that had happened in high school, they were willing to put up a fight against my new tormentor.

Something had changed. And it wasn't me.

"I just..." I sucked in a short breath, trying to shove Pierre's face out of my head. Just for a moment. "I don't understand why, after all these years, you guys are so keen on getting into my pants."

Leo snickered, and after a moment, I laughed along.

"I mean," I continued, "it's no secret that I liked Elliot. For, like, a long time." I paused to see if Leo was holding back a laugh, one more honest than the first. But he kept quiet. Maybe he was actually listening—or actually cared, for once. "But he didn't. So, did he change his mind over summer, or what?"

I could hear Leo gathering in a deep breath, as if he were about to make a difficult confession.

"Maybe we all changed our minds," he said, whispering as if he was embarrassed to be saying the words. "Or our hearts."

Hearts.

"I think you mean your sex drive," I said, trying to lighten the awkward mood. "Or your impulses."

He cracked a slight smile at that as I glanced at him. A second later, there was the sound of door hinges squeaking, and we both looked up to find Felix walking back toward us, Elliot staggering along behind him, face buried under the shadow of his hoodie. He kept his eyes down until they reached us.

I looked around at the three of them, measuring their expressions before settling back on Elliot. I couldn't help but feel a slight flutter of warmth in my belly, remembering the feeling of the sheets under my back, his lips pressed against mine. His hands. His skin.

Fuck.

This wasn't the time to think like this.

"So?" Elliot said, his voice raspier than usual. "What's the plan? What do we do with your roommate?"

Blinking, I glanced between him and Felix, waiting for a response. Instead, they looked at me.

"What?" I said. "I'm not the one who's supposed to be planning this shit out. *You* are."

"Then why are you here?" Elliot muttered, lifting his head just a little bit so that I could look into his eyes.

"Because," I drawled, "you weren't answering your phone."

His expression seemed to lighten up.

"So, what you're saying is…" he began, narrowing his eyes, "you came all the way to Powell to look for me? They didn't take you straight here?"

I nodded, as did Felix and Leo.

"Wow," Elliot whispered, a small grin flickering across his lips. Maybe there was some pride in knowing

that some desperate bitch—desperate for anything—
would make the effort to go walk a few miles to get to you.
"Okay. Well, let's see. Leo? Any ideas?"

"Well, what exactly is the goal here?" Leo replied,
turning to face me. "Is it to make her—"

"Suffer," I finished.

"Um." Leo tossed Elliot a side glance. "You're
gonna have to be more specific."

"Fine," I said. "To be specific, Vivian wants me out
of the picture. Out of her life, out of Freeman, away from
her stupid fuck buddy. I want to do the same thing. Get
her expelled."

A smirk crossed my lips at the thought.

"Gone," I finished. "Exposed for what she is. A
bully, a bitch, whatever you want to call her. Be as creative
as you like, boys."

Even though I'd told myself I wouldn't think of
him, Pierre's voice floated past me in the breeze. And I
couldn't ignore it. Not this time.

Don't change too much, Kitty Kat.

"But whatever it is," I added, heeding Pierre's
command in my head, "make sure it serves justice. Don't
do more than you need to. I just want to get the message
across that she shouldn't mess with me, or anyone else,
again."

Leo nodded, the smile on his lips expanding with
each word that came out of my mouth.

"Love it," he declared, clapping his hands together.
"I think I know what to do. Elliot?"

"Hm?" Elliot looked up at him, obviously still half-
asleep. "Yeah?"

"You think you can slip away from the big man for
the night? We got planning to do."

Elliot shrugged. "You already dragged my ass out
here, so sure."

He glanced at me, then at the ground. It occurred to me that he hadn't been warned about my knowledge of his situation at home—the financial shit that seemed to justify his attending Powell instead of a more prestigious university anywhere else in the world.

Leo nodded. "Nice."

"Let's continue this back at Powell," Felix said, spinning the car keys around his finger as he stepped around us toward the front seat. "Kat? Drop you home?"

"No way," Leo interjected, before I had the chance to reply. "She's staying. We need her input."

I glanced at Elliot to see his reaction to Leo's outburst, and he caught my eye, holding it for a long moment before pulling away as he headed around to the back seat.

"Fine," he said. "You get shotgun."

"What?" Leo said, throwing his arm up as if he were honestly exasperated. "That's cruel, man."

"That's what you get," Elliot hissed back. Before that comment, I couldn't get a read on his mood, but for the first time since I've known him, he sounded actually irritated. As if getting to share the back of a car with me was some big accomplishment.

I almost bit back some laughter, until Leo's words crept back at me.

Maybe we all changed our minds, he'd said. *Or our hearts.*

It was a nice idea. The fact that, maybe, just maybe, these bad boys had some sort of a soft spot for me under all their rough edges and even rougher actions. But it didn't add up. And I'd never believe it, even if they insisted on driving me home a thousand times over.

They were Vivian's type.

And I'd never be like her.

"I like how neither of you bothered asking Kat what she wants," Felix said, glancing at me in the rearview as we crowded into the car. "So? You wanna come with?"

I tilted my head up to gaze back at him. To be honest, hearing him say that was more refreshing than unexpected. I liked it.

"I've been awake this long," I concluded. "Why not stay up another few hours plotting with you guys?"

"Awesome," Leo said, kicking his feet up onto the dashboard. "More quality time."

I could feel Elliot's gaze on me again. I didn't know if he knew about me and Leo—about we'd almost done, and whether he even cared. It didn't matter now, anyway. Elliot couldn't expect to keep me all for himself. This was a group affair, after all.

Still, I didn't mind seeing the twinge of jealousy on his expression every time Leo looked my way or tried to make a stupid comment at my expense on the ride back to Powell. He was flirting, which terrified and piqued my interest all at once. I've seen him act this way around too many girls to count back in high school, only to see him whirl around to trip me as I passed him in the hall. But at least I'd learned to tell when Leo was interested.

He wanted more from what he'd almost gotten. More from what I could've given him.

I turned my head, looking out the window to hide the smile sneaking across my lips. There was a bit of power in being able to hold that over Leo, and I wanted it stay that way. Wished it had always *been* that way.

"And... we're back," Felix said, and I was jolted from my thoughts as we went careening over a speed bump and down into the parking garage. He parked the car, and we all got out, the sound of the slamming car doors echoing down the cavernous space like gunshots.

We had to have been the only college kids voluntarily up before 10 AM. Around here, at least.

"You know the drill," Leo said, linking arms with me to drag me toward the garage exit despite his words.

"Yeah, I know where I'm going, if that's what you mean," I muttered, jabbing him with my elbow to rid him from my arm. I meant the words to come out sounding harsher than they did, but instead, they got a little chuckle out of him. I couldn't help but mirror his smile.

"I like your fire, Kat," Leo replied, draping his arm over my shoulder. The gesture reminded me of what Pierre used to do, and this time, I let him keep it there. "You fight back."

"I didn't always," I murmured, shaking my head. If he tried to sweet-talk me one more time, he'd get a real jab to the face.

"But you are now," he said, lowering his voice as he leaned his head into the crook of my neck. Felix was a few strides ahead of us, but Elliot was lagging behind. I realized that even if he were close, he wouldn't be able to hear a word Leo was saying, not with his lips so close to my ear.

I decided to have fun with it. Payback for all those years he never liked me back.

Elliot, this is how it feels, babe.

As we neared the entrance, I curled my arm around Leo's skinny waist, and let my hand dangle at the side of his hip before lightly grasping his left butt cheek as we walked. I could feel Leo tighten his grip around my shoulders, and I knew he was smirking like an idiot. So was I.

We both knew Elliot was watching. There was no denying it.

I just wished I could see his face.

Letting go of him just long enough for us to breeze through the entrance into the dorm lobby, I glanced over my shoulder, as if making sure Elliot was still behind us, to find his eyes burning holes into the back of Leo's head.

Leo was oblivious.

We squeezed past a group of ROTC kids out on their way to training, and into the elevator. They gave us strange glances as we passed, but one of them nodded to Elliot. An awkward silence ensued as the four of us crammed into the elevator and rode up. It was silent in the hall when the elevator doors opened. Leo kept his arm around my shoulders as we walked. I made sure that we got out of the elevator ahead of Elliot.

"So," I murmured huskily, leaning into Leo's ear, "what's the plan?"

"No spoilers, sweetheart," he said, lowering his voice to my level. "Group decision."

I heard Elliot cough behind us. Instead of turning to look at him again, I looked down the hall to find Felix ahead of us once again. Man on a mission. Even if what Leo had said about changing hearts applied to him, it didn't seem to for Felix. Either he was oblivious to Leo's sudden affection for me, or honestly gave no fucks about it.

I knew that, deep down, it was very possible Leo's sudden change of mood was just all an act, that he was pretending for the sake of flipping off Elliot, using me as leverage for some sort of personal beef between the two of them. If anything, Felix's nonchalance was proof of this. He knew the truth and wasn't bothered by it.

We reached their room, and I watched as Felix shoved the door aside with his foot. He hadn't even bothered to lock it when we'd left.

They were just that feared around here. Huh.

"What the fuck?"

Felix jumped back from the door and made wild eye contact with Elliot. I narrowed my eyes at him as he pointed into the room.

"Ell," he said, "you know him?"

Elliot gave him a lopsided grin, as if he knew Felix were pulling some sort of sarcastic joke. But Felix barged into the room, and a shouting match emerged between his voice and another's.

"What the hell?" Elliot muttered, pushing between me and Leo, shoving him aside.

"That's what you get for leaving your door open," I called after him, reaching out to put a hand on Leo's shoulder. "You okay?"

"Just as I suspected," he said, cracking a grin, "he's jealous."

"And you like that?"

He shrugged. "It makes things interesting."

We followed Elliot to the room, standing outside the door and looking in to find Elliot and Felix ganging up around some kid. Even though I couldn't see his face, his voice sounded super familiar to me. It was irritating.

Squinting, I stepped into the room and past Felix and Elliot's shoulders to find myself staring, face to face, with Jason. The argument faded into silence, and he smirked at me.

Just that one look was enough for me to remember the cup full of punch splashing onto my shirt. It made me want to spit on his.

"Well, well," he said, "so it's true. You *are* their pet."

"Jesus Christ, man. Get out," Elliot practically shrieked at him, shoving Jason back to the door. Then he turned to face me. "You know each other?"

I snorted. "Barely."

"Don't be shy, Silver," Jason laughed, leaning against the doorframe. "We go way back. Two days, at least."

I rolled my eyes. The fact that he'd called me by my last name, that he even knew it, made my blood boil. I wasn't even sure that my own roommate knew my last name, let alone remembered where I was from.

Elliot and his buddies were one thing—rich bad boys with complacent sense of fashion, known for hosting parties that made city raves look tasteless. But Jason was a different sort of popular. He was a broad-shouldered jock with bad BO. Of course, his golden ratio of a face and clear skin made the cut for girls like Vivian. It didn't for me.

To me, he was a douchebag, through and through.

"What's he doing here?" Elliot pressed, stepping toward me until we were inches apart, until I knew by looking into his eyes that for once, he was angry. Really, truly, livid. At some kind of breaking point.

"Chill," Jason said. "Leave the emo chick alone. I'm here to make a deal. With you three."

"Her name's Kathleen," Leo said.

"It doesn't matter," I muttered under my breath, shooting him a look. I just wanted to hear what Jason had to say as quickly as possible. Crossing my arms, I shifted my attention back on him. "What are you talking about?"

"Look," Jason said. "I'm here on behalf of you-know-who."

"Vivian," I said, sounding bored. "Get on with it."

"Yeah. Well, here's the thing." He clapped his hands together. "It was kind of my idea for her to send that video of you and, well, this guy…" he said, glancing at Elliot, "to your mom. And it was me who, well… took it."

I raised an eyebrow at him, processing his words.

"Wait," I said, stepping toward him. "You were the one who took the video?"

He shrugged. "Not bad for my first sex tape, if I do say so myself."

My hand was already folded into a fist by the time it sliced across his cheek, and it sent his face swinging to the side. I felt strong arms pull me back.

"Hey, I'm not done!" I hissed, fighting away from Elliot and Felix's grasps. "That was for Vivian. *This* one—

" I stormed back up to Jason, and shoved my knee up into his groin, "—is for you."

"Jesus!" he shrieked, cowering back against the wall, clasping his dick through his pants. "What the hell?"

"You kinda deserved it," I heard Leo snicker from behind. For some reason, that made me whirl around, and stare him in the eyes. He was smiling.

"He did, didn't he," I said, stepping toward him. Suddenly, Leo tensed up, as if I were about to do the same to him. "And you deserve this."

Grabbing him by the back of his neck, I tugged him toward me, clamping a sloppy kiss on his lips. I remained there, pressing myself against him, waiting for him to react. Because I knew he would. And he did.

Leo relaxed, and I felt his hands gliding up my back as he tilted his head to deepen the kiss. Just as I felt a little bit of tongue grazing past bottom lip, I pulled away, and turned so that my back was to him.

Elliot and Felix were staring at me. I couldn't see the fumes spewing out of Elliot's ears, but they had to be there.

"That was…" Leo began then paused for a few long seconds. "Interesting."

Ignoring him, I stepped back toward Jason, trying not to let the butterflies in my stomach undermine the scary look I was trying to portray in my gaze.

"Just so we're on the same page," I said, "this *emo* chick is here for a reason. If you're here to make a deal, you're making it with me."

Jason threw up his hands as if in surrender.

"Okay, I'm sorry," he said. "My bad. Completely, and utterly apologetic. You have every right to—"

"Cut the bullshit. What's the deal?" I glared at him.

"Um," I heard Leo say, "I, for one, still don't understand who this guy is and how he got into our room."

Rolling my eyes, I took in a deep breath and turned back to look at him. For someone who used to act like he despised every fiber of my being, he was pretty darn adorable. Fucking blondes. I couldn't keep up the scowl.

"Fine," I said, glancing away from him. Maybe I *was* developing a crush on this kid. "Here's a quick formal introduction. Jason's a friend of Vivian's. Plays football."

"Soccer," he corrected. "Unless you're British, for which you'd be excused."

I gritted my teeth, repressing the immense urge to claw him to shreds. My tolerance for dumb humor at this point was just way below zero.

My best friend just tried to kill himself.

I didn't have the capacity to take any more BS.

"To answer the second part of your question," Jason continued hesitantly, still massaging his crotch, "Vivi asked me to follow you guys. First to the party, and then, well… I saw where you were headed after you dropped her back," he said, looking at Elliot. "Gotta say, though—your car's pretty nice, bro."

"Shut up," Elliot said.

"So you stalked us," I stated. Plain and simple. "And now my mom has a video of me having sex with the son of the guy she used to fuck, and my best friend nearly died because *somehow* he got ahold of it, too."

For the first time, Jason looked actually shocked.

"Woah," he said, blinking at me. "Didn't know all that. I just do Vivi's dirty work, I don't ask questions."

How dense could this guy be?

"I don't believe that," I growled. "I think you know more than you say. How did Pierre get the video?"

Jason couldn't have looked more like a confused child even if he tried. When I moved toward him again, he flinched.

"Jesus, please," he exclaimed, throwing his hands over his crotch. "I swear, I don't know him!" I narrowed my eyes at him. "Seriously," he pressed. "I just did what Vivian told me."

Shaking my head, I turned away from him, hoping that my anger wouldn't convert into another stream of tears and snot. I had to be strong. I had to find out the truth for Pierre.

Someone had to be brought to justice.

"We'll make sure Vivian gets what's coming to her."

The voice seemed to float out of nowhere. I turned to find Elliot's eyes staring into mine. He sounded determined, like this was now his life's work. Like he wouldn't rest until Vivian was punished.

"You're being serious," I said, my voice cracking a bit. Elliot's passion was moving.

He nodded. "I'll do anything for you."

I reached out and grabbed his arm, yanked him toward the door, and out into the hall, slamming the door shut behind us. I didn't stop there, dragging him down the hall and shoving open the first door that I saw to the left of us. A bathroom of some sort.

"Kat, what're you—"

I threw him against the wall.

"Why?" I said, standing over him. "Why are you doing this for me?"

He stared at me, the heat in his gaze mirroring my own. There was an intensity that I finally matched. All those years, this was exactly how I wish I could have looked at him.

"I like you."

The voice sounded like something out of a dream, not the mouth of my former tormentor.

"I've always liked you," he continued, his voice dripping with emotion.

Then everything made sense.

"Wait," I said, narrowing my eyes down at Elliot as he pushed himself to sit back against the wall across from me. "You're saying…"

The reason.

It was never hatred. It was never arbitrary.

It was never even because of my mom or his dad.

"All these years," I said, connecting the dots as I spoke the words, "you bullied me because you liked me?"

Elliot nodded a slow, slight nod.

I reached behind my back to lock the door, then stepped toward him.

"Look, Kat, I…" He let out a breath. "I don't know. I guess I just… didn't want you to know."

A smirk cut across my lips. God, boys were *stupid*.

"You're sick," I said. "All three of you."

Without warning, I smashed my lips against his, and my hand slipped beneath his shirt to grasp at his skin.

"Kat," he breathed, as we broke our kiss for a moment. "What're you—"

"Punishing you," I said, grabbing him by the handful of his curly black locks to pin his head against the wall. "Because that's what bullies deserve."

"Kat," he began with a twinge of a grin on his lips.

I had nothing more to say.

With one rough yank, his shirt came off, and my hands roamed his chest, my nails digging into his flesh.

I lowered my neck and began nipping at his neck before I crouched down and pulled him with me. Once I had Elliot on the floor, I settled myself down on his lap. I bucked against him, pressing my weight down against where a slight bulge began to form at his crotch. Sucking at his neckline, I reached down to undo his pants. Elliot let me do what I wanted, it was like he was my own living sex doll, like he knew he deserved this.

His pants came off in less than five seconds, and I dragged my mouth down his chest and past his belly button, nipping and licking at his hot skin as I went. Lowering my face down to his waistband, I pushed my butt farther down his thighs, and gripped his pelvis.

With my teeth, I bit down on the waistband of his boxers, and slowly, painfully, peeled it back and down. He tensed beneath me. With that, I let go. The waistband slapped back against his skin.

"Flinch again," I said, "and I'll *actually* bite you."

I used both hands to yank his boxers down and off of his legs, tossing them over my head. Next, I tore off my own skirt, casting it aside as I slid my butt back up his thighs and rested myself directly on top of his manhood.

Even though my panties still covered my pussy, I could feel his dick pushed straight up against it, throbbing, warm against my wetness. I ground down against him, hard and fast, as if fucking him for the first time all over again. Except, this time, he wouldn't get all of me. I would leave him wanting, just like I had wanted him.

"Fuck, Kat," Elliot seethed, clawing at the rim of my panties. I swatted his hands away. "Take em off."

"Says the boy who insisted he wear a condom," I muttered, remembering how on our first night alone together in his car he'd refused to fuck me pretty because he lacked protection. What a Prince Charming. "Not this time, babe."

I ground down harder against his dick, my wetness practically soaking clean through the cloth of my panties and onto his skin. I kept up the pace, rocking back and forth on him, digging my hips deeper, feeling the tip of his cock puncturing my vagina under the cotton of my panties.

"Come on, Kat," he whined again. "Stop the dry-humping."

I cracked a wicked smirk at hearing him beg and tightened my grip around his waist by pushing my legs closer against him on either side of his pelvis. Straddling him like you would a horse, squeezing tight, rubbing against him hard and fast, masturbating him.

Until suddenly, I stood up from his lap, leaving him helpless, sweaty, naked, unsatisfied.

"You want me to take em off, huh?" I said, slipping my panties down my thighs slowly, so slowly it must've killed him by the time they dropped to the floor at my ankles. "Then here."

I kicked them off and onto his lap, letting the soaked-through piece of cotton land on his dick.

"Take it as a souvenir," I said, tugging my skirt back over my legs.

He just stared up at me, stunned, like a little boy who had just gotten rejected across the face from the girl he liked.

"If you want any more of this, if you want me, then make good on what you said." With that, I turned to unlock the door and existed back into the hallway, leaving Elliot wanting.

8

I slammed the door open, and it went careening into the wall as I entered the room. Jason was still there, standing against the wall. The door nearly hit him by inches.

Walking into the center of the room, I put my hands on my hips, and scanned Leo and Felix's expressions. I'd let them think whatever they wanted about me and Elliot, about what we just did and what we didn't do. I had zero fucks left to give.

It was time for some real action.

"What's the plan?" I said, my eyes focusing back on Jason. "Your deal. What is it?"

He rubbed his hands together as if preparing to give some nerve-wracking speech. I'd never seen a jock look so much like an angsty runt.

"Okay, here's the thing," he began. "Vivi's worried that your mom is gonna freak out—"

"Already happened," I said flatly.

"Hear me out. She's worried your mom's gonna report this to the University President, and that a whole thing will come out of it that'll possibly get her expelled, or suspended, or something like that."

"Sounds great," I interrupted again. "You can leave."

"I'm not done yet," Jason muttered. I rolled my eyes. Obviously. "In order for this not to happen, she needs you to talk to your mom. Convince her not to contact the University about this."

I tapped my chin with my index finger, as if seriously considering it.

"You know what?" I said in mock enthusiasm. "I honestly don't think my mom *was* considering contacting anybody about this, but now that you mention it, it doesn't seem like such a bad idea."

I could've sworn that Jason's skin turned a shade paler than it had been before. Vivian must've had some kind of a grip on him. Maybe she'd blackmail him if he messed this up.

"This isn't funny," he said weakly. I snorted.

"It kind of is."

Jason shook his head, taking a step toward me, reaching out as if grabbing me by the shoulders and shaking me back and forth would change my sense of humor.

"It's not just Vivian who will get in trouble. I'm the one who took the video. You're the one who's *in* it," he said slowly. "And your little boyfriend... well, it's obvious he's in it, too. Even if he doesn't go to Freeman, both school administrations will get involved. It'll be bloody."

He stayed silent for a moment, allowing his words to sink in. Believe me, they were.

"You really don't want to risk getting booted out of here, do you?" he said softly. "Paying a fine, or worse? You and Elliot could go to court for this. We *all* could."

He was right. We *could* get into some big shit if someone leaked the video to any school administrators. This was a form of spying to an uncomfortable degree. And Vivian could spin the story all she wanted—that I'd asked Jason to film it, that I was prostituting myself. Who knew how sick her mind was. But I knew for a fact that, all my mom wanted to do was to pull me out of school, just as Elliot's dad had done with him. I knew my mom, and she didn't like drama.

Still, I'd told my mom that I wanted to stay. That I *had* to stay.

I told her I'd deal with this on my own.

"Okay," I said, breathing out a long sigh. "I'll do everything I can to make sure that my mom and Elliot's dad keep this a secret."

I reached out my hand. It was the least I could do to seal this kind of agreement. Hesitantly, as if expecting me to slap him across the face instead, he reached out his hand and shook mine.

"Thanks," he said. With that, he nodded to Felix and Leo before ducking back into the hallway. I could hear his footsteps as he walked—fast, light, as if he were trying his best not to run away.

I turned back to face the boys just as Elliot returned to lean against the doorframe. I ignored him, but couldn't help wondering if he'd left my panties lying there on the floor of the bathroom.

"I don't trust him," Leo said, speaking for us all. "Why the hell would he come all the way here just to say that?"

"Could've been high," Felix grunted. "Or bored."

"No," I said, narrowing my eyes at the floor as I recalled Jason's expression. "I don't know what it is, but I think you're right, Leo. There's something off. The only thing I can think of is that he didn't want us to contact the school administration first, because Vivian is going to do it her own way. She'll spin the story. Make it out to be something that it's not."

Felix nodded. "So, what do we do?"

"We get revenge," Elliot said. I turned around, daring myself to look him in the eye. His gaze locked on mine, and he waited.

"I'm listening," I said.

He glanced over his shoulder to make sure that no one was eavesdropping before slipping into the room and shutting the door behind him.

"You said you wanted justice," Elliot continued, his gaze unmoving from mine. "Look. I can't change what

I did to Pierre, and how it affected you. But I can try to change whether or not your roommate gets away with this."

I didn't have to nod, or say anything for him to know that I trusted him. He was right. He couldn't change what had happened to Pierre. But he could try to help me get revenge.

They could all try.

Seeming to read my thoughts, all of a sudden, Elliot stepped toward me and put his hand on my waist. I smirked up at him and glanced to my side at Felix and Leo.

"We need something to hold against her," Elliot continued, starting to pace the small length of the room between Felix and Leo. I couldn't help but notice how he'd somehow adopted my little mannerism. "We need some sort of dirt on her. Something that we know for sure will get her into trouble. You want her kicked off campus. Is there anything," he said, pausing his pacing to stare me dead in the eye, "*anything* you know about her that will cause that?"

My mind went blank for about a half a second before I remembered Tara pointing out the bottle of alcohol Vivian had failed to dispose of in our room. Of course, that time I'd smuggled it out to the dumpster for her, but there had to be more where that came from. I also remembered how Tara mentioned room inspections.

The only problem was, it was likely that Vivian wouldn't be the only one getting in trouble for leaving alcohol in our room. I might get the blame, too.

Maybe it was worth it.

"What's the worst that can happen if someone's caught with alcohol or drugs in the dorm?" I asked, looking to Leo.

"What? *Drugs?*" He blinked at me. "How would I know?"

"I'm asking all of you," I said, rolling my eyes. "Freeman is doing room checks this week. Probably starts sometime soon. It's random, so better safe than sorry. I'm thinking we plant some stuff on her side of the room and wait for the authorities to deal with her."

"So, we're setting her up," Elliot said. "The issue is, worst comes to worst, she has to take an online alcohol safety course and gets off easy. Drugs ... I don't know about that."

He was right. Getting caught drinking in the dorm was old news for most RAs. Knowing the other shit they dealt with on a day to day basis, getting partiers to clean up after themselves was probably the least of their concerns. Find a kid shooting up heroin or selling crack in the dorms? That was a whole other ball game.

Suddenly, I had a bright idea.

"I know someone who might know," I said, pulling out my phone to search for Tara's contact. "His name's Kenny. From my first impression of him, he's a total hipster. Smokes like grass is his air. But maybe he's a bit more hardcore."

I scrolled through my contacts to text Tara, but paused before sending the message. I didn't have time to wait for a reply. Instead, I called her up, and pressed the phone to my ear, waiting as her ringer went off.

"Hey," she said. I could tell she was trying to make her voice sound less groggy than I knew it was. "You're ... up?"

"Yeah, sorry," I said, chuckling more to myself than to her. Amidst all the chaos, my sense of time had become sort of irrelevant. "Didn't mean to wake you."

"No, it's fine," she yawned. "What's up?"

"Do you have Kenny's number? I need to ask him something."

There was silence on the other end of the line, and I was worried something might've happened between the two of them after I'd left that night until she said, "Yeah, of course. Can I ask why?"

For a moment, I was hesitant to tell her exactly why I needed his contact info. I mean, what was I supposed to say—I need to see if he can give me some drugs so that I can hide it in my roommate's hellhole of a closet?

Maybe that wasn't enough.

Maybe we needed to gather more info before making the first move. That's what Elliot had suggested—find out something about Vivian that's true, that would really get her into trouble without risking our own somewhat bruised reputations from worsening.

"Here's the thing," I said, lowering my voice. "Vivian's put me in a tough position. I can't tell you everything right now, but … would you want to help?"

There was another long pause, and then, "I've got nothing better to do."

I smiled. "Great. Can I meet you at your door in a half an hour, or so?"

"Sure." I could hear her smiling from the other end of the line, too. "This better be juicy."

I hung up the phone feeling good. If I knew anything about Tara at all from the last couple of days I'd gotten to feel her out, it was that she hated Vivian's guts just as much, if not, more than I did. Even better, she knew Vivian well. If there was anyone who knew what it'd take to push her buttons, it'd be her.

"Whoa, wait," Leo said. "*Now* what're we doing?"

"My friend said she'll help out," I replied, stepping toward the door. "Long story short, she's got some good beef with Vivian, and probably an even better idea of what to do about her." I nodded to his flip-flops. "I suggest you guys put on some better clothes."

"Why?" He grinned back at me. "These won't cut it at Freeman?"

I glanced down at them. "The fact that they're designer-brand might."

"That's what I like to hear," Leo said, that puppy-dog grin still strung tight across his lips as he bounded over to the door to hold it open for me. "Milady."

"Shut up," Elliot said, pushing past him through the door before I could even take a step. Even if I hated his guts, he could've at least appreciated the fact that I'd gone all the way with him at least once. That was more than Leo could say.

He was as stubborn in his jealousy as he was jealous. I wasn't used to this—guys drooling all over me, or rather, huffing and puffing.

It was hot.

"I'll drive," Felix said, stepping out after me. "I don't think Ell's in the mindset for keeping us safe tonight."

"The sun is up," Leo sang, shuffling out the door last, once again not bothering to close it behind us.

"Whatever," Felix yawned, tossing and catching his car keys again. "If I'm tired, it's nighttime."

It took us a few minutes to get back into the parking garage, as the elevator stopped more frequently as students entered and left at every other floor. Finally, we'd made it to the lobby, and back into Felix's low BMW. The ride to Freeman was silent. I couldn't speak for them, but I was lost in my thoughts—of Pierre, of the last few years of high school, marveling at how I'd managed to get myself into a situation where I was packed into a car with three of the hottest boys of high school when only a few months ago they'd barely give me a second look.

The past few days had to be a dream, or at times, a nightmare.

"Just pull up here," I told Felix as he drove into the circular driveway. There was a group of students hanging out around the steps to the entrance of the dorm building, and their eyes followed us as we parked the car. "There's a parking lot around the side of the building. Just drop us off here."

"Gotcha," Felix said. "Meet me inside?"

"Here," I said, handing him my student ID. The kids at the front desk had already learned to recognize my face, due to the fake period stain—the one thing I could thank Vivian for. I wouldn't need to show it to them. "Show this when you walk in and come to the fourth floor. We'll be in room 434."

Leo, Elliot and I got out of the car and headed straight toward the entrance. A few of the students around us fell into fits of whispers and giggles, but most just stared. On any normal day, I would've figured they were just swept away by my companions' toxic good looks, or the fact that they were being seen with me.

But this was not a normal day. I was running on less than an hour of sleep, but even I could tell that these kids were judging us. That they knew more.

"Hey," Leo called out to one of them as we parted ways with Felix. "Whatcha lookin' at?"

They immediately cast their gazes to the sidewalk and began whispering amongst themselves. Vivian must've started some fresh rumors, and I honestly couldn't care.

In a few hours, she'd be done for. I just had to keep that in mind.

In a few hours, my life would be off to a good start. For good.

We strode into the lobby like the biggest, baddest clique any high school had ever seen, and I didn't need to say anything to the front desk kids as we slipped by. Yes, I did drag these two boys out of bed, and yes, they were my guests, and no, you can't do anything to stop me from bringing them into the dorm.

This is what it must've felt like to be Elliot Lancaster.

Once we reached Tara's room, her door had already been opened. I heard a voice from inside, but it didn't sound like hers. It sounded more like a recording. I motioned for the guys to stay behind me and knocked lightly a few times on the door. When she didn't answer, I pushed it open a little further, and peeked inside.

Tara was on the floor, leaning against her bed, face clasped in her hands. Crying.

"Oh my God," she said, lifting her head suddenly, startling me more than I must've startled her. "Sorry, I... Come in."

"What..." I pushed open the door and rushed in, crouching down beside her. "Tara, what happened?"

If it was Vivian, I swore...

"It was her," she stuttered, as if reading my thoughts. "Yeah. Big surprise, right?"

I shook my head, reaching out to stroke the hair out of her face as she sniffled in some snot. "What did she do to you?"

If it had anything to do with me, I was going to ram my skull into the nearest hard surface. Not that it mattered. How was I supposed to ask Tara for help with someone who was already making her life hell? Who'd already *been* making her life hell?

Perhaps that would be an incentive.

"Look, you don't have to tell me if you don't want to," I said, and waited a moment. "But I think you should."

She looked up at me, pausing her shuddering shoulders and sniffling to look back and forth between my eyes, as if realizing who I was, realizing that I wasn't there to hurt her. Seeing her like this made me beyond angry.

I was disappointed in the whole of humanity. Could there be such a feeling?

How someone could make a girl as sweet as Tara break down like this was beyond my comprehension.

No. I *wished* it was beyond my comprehension.

"It's okay," Tara sniffled, taking in a deep breath. "She… must've found out about my stupid little crush on Eric, because she started something. Something between me and you."

I shook my head, not understanding her words. "Between… me and you?"

"It was Kenny," she said, breaking out into another short-lived, but strong round of tears. "She saw him leave my room this morning, and she knew that you'd been with us. He must've let slip that I had a thing for Eric. She told him. Told all his friends. And some rumors about how me, Kenny, and you had a threesome." She said the last word as if they were hot garbage on her tongue, which they might as well have been. "Everyone thinks I'm some psycho. That *we're* the ones who are whores. She's turned us into a fat joke. And everyone believes her."

Fuck.

I wanted to burst out laughing. If only Vivian knew—threesomes weren't my thing. Foursomes were more like it.

Still, I couldn't hold back. Not anymore.

Mess with me? That was one thing. I was used to being kicked around. I had Elliot to thank for that.

But Tara? Kenny? Pierre? My friends, all of them, were pure souls. Innocent as they come. They didn't deserve shit like this.

I got off the floor and spun around to face the door.

"Kat?" I heard Tara call. But it was too late.

I was already charging down the hall, had whipped my key card out in less than a second, and slammed it against the door handle. My door clicked open, and I flung it aside to find Vivian giggling away on the floor in her skimpy pair of athletic shorts that she used as pajama bottoms and hot-pink hoodie.

"Wow," she laughed, her lips curling into a smirk only the devil could pull off on a good day. "Look at what the cat dragged i—"

I smacked her across the face.

Her head swung to the side. Her friend's laughter immediately stopped.

She turned back, glare colder than ice.

"Don't you dare," I said, before she could open her pretty, pouty lips. "Don't you ever hurt Tara like that. She hasn't done anything to you. Nothing."

She simply stared at me, all expression vanished from her face. She was shocked. Didn't think someone like me, a frail girl with loud makeup and a low tolerance to alcohol, could ever stand up to someone like her.

A prick.

An egotistic, insecure bitch. Yeah, I've met the type before, in boy-form.

If I could stand up to them, I could stand up to her, twofold.

"You ruin people's lives, you know?" I said, my voice shaking like it was the end of the world, and I was standing at its fracturing edge. I couldn't help the tears from burning past my eyelids. A torrential rain was about to pour down my cheeks. "Maybe you don't know it, but there's something called the motherfucking *butterfly* effect. Sometimes, your actions *actually* have consequences. In your case—"

"Kat," I heard someone say.

I turned around to find Felix standing at the door, watching me with a deep look of concern in his eyes. Probably just came to make sure I hadn't started a catfight. Ha.

Three days too late.

Felix nodded to motion for me to step back out into the hall. Clamping my jaw tight, I relented, picking myself off the floor before storming back out of the room and slamming the door shut behind us. But I didn't go far. I planted myself into place right outside my room, crossing my arms as I looked at Felix.

"What?" I snapped.

He let out a rugged sigh. "Kat, there's something you might wanna see."

Oh God. "What now?"

He shoved his hands in his wide front pockets, and scanned the hallway as if to make sure we weren't being overheard, or spied on. Both were highly likely possibilities at this point.

"When Jason came to talk to us," he said, resting his hand lightly on my shoulder to gently guide me away from the door, "I think he was trying to help."

"What?" I repeated, trying my best to keep my voice down. Trying and failing. "What do you mean?"

The rest of the boys seemed to have disappeared into Tara's room, and in the quiet, we could hear their voices muttering back and forth through the closed door. Felix ignored it, sucking in a deep breath before stepping closer to me so that no one would hear the conspiracy theory he was about to spill.

Might as well have been one. Jason, helping?

He was the one who *took* the damn video.

"When he said not to bring the video to the school's attention," he began slowly, trying to choose his words wisely, "I think he was speaking between the lines, if that makes sense. I think... he wanted us to bring it to the school's attention. At the least, that's what he was suggesting. Because maybe he knew that Vivian was going to do it, unless we did it first..."

His voice trailed off on purpose, it seemed, as if he were waiting for me to fit the rest of the pieces together.

"You sound like you actually paid attention in high school," I muttered, which managed to crack a smile in his usually stony, I-mean-business-and-no-bullshit expression.

"Between the lines... Okay. You're saying that he was giving us a warning. *Foreshadowing*, if you will."

He laughed at that, to my surprise. "Sure, Kathleen," he said. "Foreshadowing."

Chills went down my spine as he said that—my name.

No one ever just said my actual name like that, as if it were as casual as Kat, or Sam, or even AJ. He made it sound like he'd been saying it all his life, as if he'd been practicing, at the very least.

I liked it.

"Anyway," he continued, leaning a little more toward me, lowering his voice so I was forced to do the same. "I think he wanted to help without being obvious about it. Maybe Vivian did want him to come tell us not to bring this to the school's attention, but the way he'd said it... I don't know. It just seemed like he was hinting that that was the exact thing we s*hould've* done."

"But how can you know that?" I asked.

"Because," Felix said, and let out a hefty sigh. "Vivian already *brought* it to their attention."

I narrowed my eyes at him.

Just then, I got a notification on my phone, feeling it vibrate in my hand. Gulping, I flipped my phone over in my hand to find that I got an email in my school inbox. I swiped it open, read its contents, then looked back up at Felix.

"You've gotta be kidding," I said, re-reading the message just in case I was imagining it. As if my imagination could be responsible for any of this. "It's an email from the Office of Student Life. They're summoning me to some kind of meeting."

"Fuck," Felix breathed.

"They want me there at three tomorrow." I shook my head, putting my phone away. "I don't understand.

How could Vivian bring this up to them? How could she defend herself?"

Felix shrugged, but it was a sad, almost defeated gesture. For once, he didn't know. "I guess we'll find out."

Again, I narrowed my eyes at him. "We?"

He pulled out his phone and showed me the screen. "I got the same email. All of us did. Me, Leo, Ell."

Shaking my head, I pushed past him to head back to Tara's room. I had no space in my head to deal with this meeting right now. When the time came, I'd go, and give it my all. But I couldn't preoccupy my thoughts with it right now. Tara was sobbing her eyes out, and Vivian was asking for sweet, sweet revenge.

"Hey," I said, pushing the door open slightly to find it was still unlocked. Tara was still crouched on the floor, and Elliot and Leo were leaning awkwardly against the wall to her side, feeding her a tissue box. Her eyes seemed to light up, a small spark of hope, as I walked in.

"I hope you beat her up," she gurgled. That evoked a giggle from both of us. "Hope you made her cry like a baby."

"Not quite," I said, stooping down to her level. Once Felix had shut the door behind us, I settled down on the floor across from her. "Look," I began, "we can still get back at her."

"How?"

I looked up at Elliot. "Did you tell her anything?"

He shook his head. "Told her to wipe her face up."

I rolled my eyes, turning back to Tara.

"We have an idea, inspired by that little stunt you told me to pull with the bottle of Vodka, or whatever it was that was chilling in my room earlier. You said there are room checks coming up. What if we planted some hard drugs—something sketchy as hell—into her side of the room?"

I watched her expression carefully to see if she was following me through her curtain of bleary tears. She was, it seemed, as a frown formed on her lips.

"Like I told you before," she began, "both of you can get into trouble. Even if you didn't right away, she could always allege that you were the one who put the stuff there.

I smirked. "Not if I'm not there to begin with."

Tara's eyebrows drew together. I looked to my side to find that Elliot and Leo had the same confused expression. "What?" they said at the same time.

I got to my feet.

"My mom wanted to pull me out of school," I started explaining, "when all this shit started happening. I could still take her up on it. Classes haven't even started yet, and refunds on tuition are still valid through the next two weeks. It'd be believable. If I pretended to leave, then how could they blame me for something I wasn't there to do?"

I looked from one expression to the next as everyone's faces contorted from confusion to eager nods. This could happen. It all started to seem real—not only to me, but to them.

The battle had just begun.

"Room inspections are day after tomorrow," Tara said, wiping some snot from her upper lip with her sleeve. She cleared her throat. "If you can get out by today, have all your things removed, then yeah. It could work."

I smiled at her, and she smiled back. "That could definitely work," I replied, "considering all I brought with me was a suitcase with some toiletries and a few changes of now-ruined clothes."

Ah, the perks of being on a budget.

"Yeah," Felix said, as if coming to his own conclusion. "The only person you'd have to convince is your roommate. No one else has to know you're really just staying here."

I nodded. "Exactly."

"Ooh," Tara said, sitting up all of a sudden. I was glad this was able to take her mind off of what Vivian had done to her, even if it had to do with Vivian herself. "You can stay in my room for the next couple of nights, if you want."

"Sure, thanks," I said, feeling my chest buzz up with nerves. This was actually happening. "Do you think Kenny would like to be in on this?"

Tara smirked, and for the first time since I'd met her, her expression seemed actually wicked.

"*Hell* yes," she said. "He wants revenge on this bitch just as much as I do. Plus, he's got more LSD than he knows what to do with. I think he can spare some to stuff under your roommate's mattress."

I couldn't help but laugh a little at the image of Kenny dashing into my room with a conspicuous-looking package only to dash out seconds later with nothing but a sloppy grin on his face. I looked at Elliot and the boys, and motioned to bring them out into the hall.

"Can I chat with you guys outside for a quick sec?" I smiled at Tara. "I'll be right back."

They followed me out into the hall without a word, and we made a tight circle a few yards away from Tara's room.

"This is perfect," I said. "We go to this meeting tomorrow with the Dean of Students, and the day after, we get our revenge."

"Question," Felix said, holding up his index finger. "What if what happens at that meeting tomorrow affects the plan? What do we do?"

"Oh, shit," Leo exclaimed. "Wait—do you think your roommate's gonna be in that meeting?"

I nodded.

"Considering that *she* was the one who brought it to the school's attention, I wouldn't be surprised," I answered. "But it works in our favor. While we're all at the meeting, Kenny can duck into my room and plant the drugs. Since all four of us will be in that same meeting, they can't suspect that we were the ones to have done it."

Felix clapped. "We have a plan, everybody."

"We sure do," I said, allowing a big smile to grow across my face. "Any final concerns?"

The three boys looked around at each other before their gazes settled back onto me. For once, I was the one in charge. For once, I had their fate, all of our fates, in my own hands.

9

"Kathleen Silver?"

I looked up from my phone to find that the secretary had appeared back around the corner and was motioning for me to follow her inside like a nurse at a doctor's office. I'd been waiting outside the Office of Student Life for about twenty minutes, drumming my fingers against my thigh as I went over the morning's events in my head.

I'd moved all my stuff—that is, one suitcase—over to Tara's after the boys had gone back to Powell last night, and told Vivian that I was going to be transferring. She'd simply shrugged, which scared me more than it should've. Maybe I'd expected more of a reaction from her. It was as if she knew I was lying, as if everything was going according to plan. According to *her* plan.

I rose from my seat and followed the secretary to a door a few yards from the front desk of the Office. It was a conference room. She let me inside, and I was greeted by six pairs of eyes—Elliot, Leo, Felix, Vivian, Jason, and the mysterious Dean of Students herself.

"Kathleen," she said, and gestured to the seat opposite of her. "Please."

Forcing a flat smile onto my face, I moved toward the chair, watching out the corner of my eye as the secretary shut the door behind me. I unstrapped my purse from my shoulder and slung it over the back of the chair before settling in. Leo and Felix sat on either side of me, while Elliot and Vivian sat across from each other. I was directly opposite to the Dean, who sat at the head of the conference table.

"My name is Pat O'Donnell," the Dean said. "I spoke to you guys in a few email blasts over the summer. I'm sure you remember."

She cracked a smile as if that was the funniest joke she'd crafted in weeks, and I almost felt bad when no one reciprocated the smile. After a slow, awkward moment of silence, the Dean folded her hands on the table in front of her, and leaned forward a bit in her seat.

"So, let's cut to the chase," she said, "and review the facts of the matter. From what I know, Vivian supplied the Office of Student Life with this video clip. I assume you are all aware of this, and the content of the clip?"

Everyone nodded as if in some bored, trance-like state. Nobody wanted to be here, and yet, we all did. I'd shown up to defend myself against whatever story Vivian had concocted about me and Elliot, and that was a good enough reason to subject myself to this kind of social torture.

I glared at Vivian, but she didn't seem to notice— or chose not to. She kept her eyes straight ahead, smirking at Jason, who sat across from her beside Elliot. Jason seemed to force a grin back, only to toss a side glance toward Elliot, who sat sulking in his chair like a fourth grader in time-out.

"Vivian," the Dean said, turning to my arch-nemesis. "Would you like to explain why you sent this video clip to the Office?"

"Sure, Ms. O'Donnell," Vivian peeped, smiling like a motherfucking waitress at a Hooters. "My friend, Jason here, was at a party at the Lancaster's place, and filmed a sex tape of these two," she practically spat, shifting her gaze to me and Elliot, "with only one person's consent."

"What?" I couldn't help but let out a maniacal laugh. "And whose consent would that be?"

Vivian nodded to Elliot. He didn't look up from the surface of the table. In fact, it looked like he'd shoot himself right then and there, if he could.

"He asked Jason to do it," Vivian continued, looking to Jason. "Isn't that right?"

I shook my head. I couldn't let her continue spewing lies.

"*You* asked him," I stated. "Not, Elliot, *you.*"

Vivian cocked an eyebrow at me.

"Oh, yeah? Then why would Elliot send it to me?"

"What?" Elliot and I both said at the same time as I jumped to my feet.

"You did this?" I whispered. I was too angry to feel the tug of tears. My whole body went numb as I stared at him, into him.

"No, I... I-"

"He sent it to me," Vivian interrupted, "and told *me* to pretend I was the one who told Jason to film it. He even offered to pay me to do it. Like I don't do my research." She snorted. "I know who you are, Lancaster. Everyone does. And we all know that you don't have *shit* to pay me off with. Not anymore. So when I got this sex tape, I sent it to the Office of Student Life because receiving that stupid video is kind of sexual *harassment.*"

Now, it was time for me to interrogate Elliot. That mother-*fuck*er.

I couldn't believe this.

I couldn't believe him.

Who could I believe?

"Why would you do this?" I ground out. "Did you have Jason tape this video for the sole purpose of sending it to Pierre and ruining his life. Ruining mine."

When I looked to Jason, I saw him flinch, casting his gaze down to the floor.

Shaking my head, I settled back in my chair, and almost threw my legs up onto the surface of the table to stretch out. I didn't drink, but fuck, I *needed* something calm my system before it exploded.

"She's lying!" Elliot finally blurted. "I wouldn't, I would never!"

"Really?" Vivian butted in again. "Because from what I understand, you've always been a bully to poor Kathleen here. It seems like this is right up your alley."

The funny thing was, it all made sense. Elliot was diabolical. I knew it from the start. If things didn't go his way, then, well, he'd *make* it go his way. It was so like him. Plus, how would Jason know that Elliot was bringing me to his cousin's place if Elliot didn't tell him himself?

I didn't know what to say.

"I just want to say," the Dean interrupted, breaking me out of my half-daze, "it's a Class H felony in North Carolina to disclose a sexual image of someone with the intent to humiliate or harass an individual." Suddenly, all eyes were on her. She took in a slow breath, her milky gaze resting on me, and then Elliot. "Mr. Lancaster, are you aware that Powell and Freeman are sister schools? And that we still share the same codes of conduct?"

Elliot's eyes simply flicked up at her.

"Don't think that just because you don't go to the same institution as these young ladies," the Dean continued, gesturing to me and Vivian, "that you won't get punished. I know exactly what Powell's administration will have to say about this, and it's not going to be pretty."

For the first time since I'd arrived on the scene, Elliot moved—throwing up his arms, he pushed back his chair as if to make a mad dash for the door.

"Fine, get them involved, but I'm not the one at fault here." He glared at Vivian. "This bitch will get what's coming to her."

"Mr. Lancaster!" The dean chided. Elliot sank back down to his chair. "Is that's all you have to say?" the Dean pressed.

"Yeah."

She turned to Jason, whose eyes hadn't moved from the floor. "So, it seems we have two sides pointing fingers at each other with you in the middle. Do you care to clear the air with your side of the story?"

Jason swallowed before looking up to the dean and then over to Vivian, who looked like she was going to bore a hole through his head with her glare alone.

"Vivian paid me to do it," he admitted then went silent. His eyes were back to the floor and he wasn't going to dare look Vivian in the eye again.

"How dare you!" Vivian shrieked. She shot up from her chair and I was sure she was about to pounce on Jason. "That's not what we talked about!"

The dean stood, positioning herself between Vivian and Jason. "Vivian, please sit down. You don't want assault added to your list of transgressions."

Vivian huffed then slowly sat down. I watched as she worked her jaw and I could practically hear her teeth grinding.

"Now, before we go on…" the Dean began, almost reluctantly. This had to have been the most amusement she'd had throughout her whole career at Freeman. "Why don't we schedule times to meet one-on-one? Now that I've gotten the full picture, I think it's best that I meet with each one of you separately to dig a little deeper into the situation. I believe we have the generally gist of what's going on, but I'll need further details before punishments are decided."

No one responded, except for a few shrugs here and there. The dean looked between us and opened her mouth to speak when someone's ringtone broke the silence. The dean put up a finger, indicating that we should wait for a moment as she took her phone and stepped out of the room.

"So… it wasn't you?" I asked, turning to Elliot. "You didn't plan this?"

"No." I came out like a whisper. "And I'm sorry all this happened." He gestured around at the situation we were in. "And I'm sorry about Pierre."

"Me too," Leo chimed in.

"Me too… too," Felix added.

I smiled at the three of them, relieved that they hadn't been involved, but also angry that I had actually believed Vivian, even if it was only for a moment.

Vivian.

That liar.

That *bitch*.

I turned to Vivian, a rage suddenly boiling up from inside. Just like everything else that had happened since I arrived, this was *her* fault. I could feel the flush rising in my cheeks and my fingernails digging into my palms as I balled my hands into fists. I was ready to jump from my seat and wail on her.

"Don't," a voice came from beside me, along with a soft hand on my shoulder. "It isn't worth it."

"Isn't worth it? *Isn't worth it?*" I hissed turning to the voice and meeting Elliot's eyes. The corner of his lip turned up in a kind of half smirk and he shook his head.

I wanted to push him away. I wanted to tackle Vivian to the ground and yell and scream and punch until all of the rage inside of me was gone. Until what she did to Pierre was avenged.

"Excuse me, Miss Russo," the Dean practically growled as she re-entered the room. "Please come with me, there is an issue with your room."

Vivian's expression went cold. She looked around the room, blinking as if she was seeing everyone for the first time, as if it'd finally hit her that she was in trouble of some shape or form.

"Vivian?" the Dean asked.

Vivian rose from her seat, cursing under her breath. In less than two seconds she'd gathered up her stuff and was headed toward the door.

"You may all go, though we will be in contact to follow up," the dean said before following Vivian out, the door slamming shut behind her.

I looked at Elliot. We both knew what that phone call had to be about. All four of us did. They must've done room inspections early. How convenient.

I dashed out of the room and as I headed back to the dorm building, I pulled out my phone and searched for a text or a call from Kenny. There was nothing. Not even from Tara. Part of me wondered if he'd chickened out, or simply forgotten about the whole stunt, until I felt a hand on my shoulder.

I whirled around to find myself face to face with him.

"Kenny," I said, drawing my brows together. "What're you doing? Did you... you know..."

He nodded quickly, handing my room key back to me. "I went to your room with the stuff, but when I got there—"

"Oh, shit," I said, putting two and two together. "Did they check the rooms before you could get there?"

He shook his head. "No, it's not that. It's kinda funny actually," he laughed, scratching the back of his head. "When I was looking for a place to hide the stuff, well... I didn't *have* to." He raised his eyebrows, his lips curling into the goofiest grin I'd ever seen. Made me wonder if instead of hiding the drugs in Vivian's stuff, he'd decided to use it himself.

"Okay, Kenny," I said, rolling my eyes. "Spit it out."

"She already *has* shit in her room," he exclaimed, rubbing his hands together as if it were the most amusing thing. "Like, loads. We didn't *need* to plant drugs in her room. She already had enough."

A smile slowly crept onto my lips, and I blew out a sigh of relief.

"Wow, okay," I said, running a hand through my hair. I froze for a second, and then, the two of us burst out in laughter.

"Seriously," he said. "She's, like, overflowing with ecstasy and shit."

"No way," I laughed, imagining Vivian packing Ziploc bags filled with grams and pills behind her parents' shoulders to bring to college with her. "No fucking way. This is fantastic."

"It's weird, that's for sure," Kenny admitted, shaking his head. "She did our dirty work for her."

"Takes off the guilt, I guess," I replied, nodding toward the dorm building. "Let's go find out what happened."

"What do you mean?"

Kenny followed me as I started off again toward the building.

"I was in a meeting with Vivian," I explained, unsure of how much he knew about the situation. Probably nothing, considering I hadn't really told Tara. If anything, he figured it had to do with the rumor Vivian spread about the three of us. "The dean got a call all of a sudden and then pulled Vivian out of the meeting due to an issue with our room. I assumed she'd gotten a call from Housing about the room checks and that they'd found something."

"You're probably right," Kenny agreed.

We pushed our way through the doors and into the lobby. Suddenly, I stopped in my tracks. Vivian and the dean were standing at the front desk, talking quietly with one of the receptionists. Vivian looked completely distraught, bunching her red hair up with one hand as she reached out to grab a packet of paper with the other. We slowed our steps as we passed, and she gave us a quick glance, nothing more than acknowledging our presence.

It made sense now, the fact that her room was so messy.

She probably figured that there was no way the RAs would comb through it all, but it probably only made her look more suspicious.

I almost felt... bad for her.

Almost.

Just before we turned the corner, I watched as she went rifling through the packet of papers, appearing to be signing her name here and there. Then, she took out her student ID, and slid it across the desk.

Ouch.

Somehow, I felt a pit in my stomach.

Sure, these kids had gotten a thrill out of trying to make *my* life miserable, no matter what their motivation had been—and yet, returning the favor didn't calm the anger that I'd bottled up in me for so long. The idea of getting them into trouble was exciting, but once it happened, it didn't feel enough.

Maybe justice wasn't enough.

"How's Tara doing?" I asked Kenny as we got into the elevator. "Did she tell you what happened?"

"About what your roommate said about us?" He blew out a puff of air. "Yeah. She's twisted."

Thankfully, we were alone the whole ride up, so we didn't have to endure the side glances and whispers of kids who had heard Vivian's little interpretation of our innocent game night. We got off on my floor and headed for Tara's room.

"It doesn't bother you?" I asked him, lowering my voice as we drew closer. "The fact that Vivian said those things?"

"Of course, it does," he said, but his voice seemed distant. "But I'm more angry about it because of how it affects Tara. It's not fair to her. I can be a total weirdo, but Tara? She's sweet, and nice, and—"

I looked at him with a smile.

"—and doesn't deserve to be treated like that," he said, blushing. He dipped his head toward the floor as we came to Tara's door, and that smirk didn't fade from his face, though his voice lowered to a whisper. "I really hope she didn't hear that."

"Why?" I giggled. "I think she should."

God, they were so cute together. If only I was capable of having normal crushes that turn to normal relationships.

I knocked on Tara's door a couple times and stepped back to wait as I heard footsteps shuffle over. She unlocked the door and opened it to reveal herself with a fresh face of makeup and a revitalized grin. Seeing her okay again gave me hope—if this girl could get through four years plus of Vivian Russo, so could I.

"Hey," she said. "Come in. How'd *it* go?"

She emphasized the word *it* as she glanced at Kenny. We scurried into her room and she shut the door with an eager push before jumping back onto her mattress.

"Well," I said, looking at Kenny, "I think she's gone. For good."

Suddenly, Tara narrowed her eyes at Kenny, and pushed herself off the bed, barreling up to him.

"Dude, what the *fuck*?" she whispered harshly, snatching a plastic grocery bag from his hand. I hadn't even noticed that it was there, and now, I barely needed to guess at its contents. "This doesn't look empty!"

"Because!" he said, as if that was more than enough justification. "She didn't need it! She already *had* shit in her room."

Tara's face crumbled from utter terror to pure, blissful relief as she tore the bag from Kenny's hand and peered inside to find it chock full of… well, I'd never know.

"Jesus, Kenny," she cackled, putting a hand over her chest as she stumbled back over to her bed. "Were you just carrying it around campus like this?"

Kenny's expression scrunched up as if he were actually mulling over the question. "Uh, well, yes?"

Tara shook her head, clicking her tongue in mock disapproval. "And somehow, he didn't get caught. What a beast."

"Thank you."

I smiled, looking between the two of them as if I were the one falling in love until Tara let out a long breath. "So, she's one of us?"

"Apparently so," Kenny answered. "Isn't that wild?"

"Completely." Tara stared into space, shaking her head slowly as if seeing something we couldn't, like she was recalling an odd dream. "In all the years I've known her, I *never* would've expected this. So, she still got caught?"

I nodded. "I assume so. We saw her down at the front desk with the dean. Looked like she was signing herself out of the dorm."

Tara's eyes widened. "What? Really?"

"Yep." I nodded and made a slow round around her room, looking at her stacks of books, photographs and generic university-dispensed furniture for a sign of disturbance. But there looked to have been none. "What about you? Did they go through your stuff?"

She shook her head.

"Nah. I think I'm scheduled for tomorrow. Speaking of which," she said, a sly smile spreading on her lips, "I was wondering if I could store some of my stuff in your room for a few hours? You know, just because your place has already been cleaned out…"

I raised an eyebrow at her. "By *stuff*, you mean…"

She copied my expression. "Oh, you know exactly what I mean."

"Sure thing," I replied, rolling my eyes. "Not to change the subject, but how are you holding up? Last time I saw you, you were, you know…"

"Shedding tears?" Tara finished, flipping her hair over her shoulder as if crying were the most blasé thing to do with one's bodily functions since breathing. "I'm a seasoned sobber, and I clean up quickly. I'm fine. Thanks for checking in."

"Good to hear it," I said. "I… think."

Tara slid herself off her bed and skipped over to her closet. "Your things are in here," she said, lugging my suitcase out of the tight space. "And then some."

She took a shoebox off of the top shelf and tucked it under her arm. Once I took the suitcase, I followed her back out into the hall, and we headed to my room. I unlocked the door to find Vivian's side of the room just as chaotic as usual, except for the fact that she was absent. I tossed my suitcase back onto the floor.

"Watch this," Tara said, pulling my desk chair out from under my desk. She stepped onto it and hoisted the shoebox up toward the ceiling. Before going any further, she put her index finger against her lips. "Shh!"

"Ah, I see what's going on here," I said as she pushed one hand up against a square ceiling tile to shift it aside. Smirking, she stuffed the box up into the ceiling, and carefully replaced the tile. Before hopping back down to the floor, she pointed her finger at the tile closest to the wall, and counted the number of tiles to the one above her. "Three from the windows and five from the wall. Remember that."

"You remember that," I laughed. "I'm not going to stick my hand up there any time soon."

I felt my phone vibrate in my pocket, and I couldn't help but shudder as I swiped open the screen. I'd expected to find some venomous text from Vivian, or possibly my mom, considering the Dean might've contacted her about everything going on. Instead, it was a package notification from the front desk of the building.

The rest of my clothes.

"What're you smiling about?" Tara asked, bouncing over to me to peer over my shoulder. "Is it that Leo kid? He was cute."

I snorted and decided to ignore her mention of Leo. I needed to forget about the three of them, just for a few hours. Heck, even a few minutes would do it for me. I needed a break. Mentally.

Emotionally.

"I have to head down to the mailroom," I said. "I got a package. Should be my clothes."

"Oh, awesome," Tara said. "That means I get my leggings back!"

We exited my room, and Tara decided to stick around with Kenny for a bit in her room while I'd go to pick up my package. I couldn't help but feel genuinely happy, a bit giddy, as I glided down to the lobby floor in the elevator. This was a good sign. I was here to stay.

If I could get through Vivian, I could get through anything. I'd earned my place here at Freeman in the most abstract way possible.

The line for the mailroom was pretty short. From what I'd overheard from conversations with upperclassmen, the lines could snake out the door of the lobby on the worst days. I was the fifth person in line. I leaned against the wall, watching students come in and out of the lobby doors.

"Kat?"

I turned around to find that someone had joined the line behind me. Elliot.

"Hey," I said, smiling at him out of decency more than anything else. "How's it going?"

"Uh, you know," he said, leaning against the wall beside me, leaning in toward me a little bit so that our shoulders were almost touching. "Just anticipating my classes to start."

I snickered. "How riveting."

He kept his gaze on me, smiling with his eyes more than anything else.

"So, uh…" he said, lifting his hand to scratch at the back of his neck, "there's this party…"

I almost wanted to throw up on him.

"Oh, yeah?" I choked out. "Count me out."

"Wait, it's not like *that* kind of a party," he said, nearly reaching out to grab onto my shoulders. The person at the front of the line left the desk, and I shuffled forward as the line became shorter.

"I don't want anything to do with your parties," I muttered, trying to keep my voice level. I'd had enough attention drawn onto me for one day.

"Kat," he sighed. "Seriously. I'm sorry about how things have been—"

His gaze turned grim, and for a moment, it seemed as if he were on the brink of shedding some sort of a tear.

"Look," he said softly, keeping his eyes locked onto mine. "I'm sorry. Just… give me another shot. Please?"

Oh, shit. Now he was begging.

Pleading.

The line moved up again, and I took another couple of steps forward. After a moment of staring at the desk, pretending to find it incredibly fascinating compared to Elliot's face, I turned back to him.

"Okay," I said. "What type of party is this, exactly?"

The smile that gushed across his face was big enough to melt the heart of any Disney princess.

"It's more of a small gathering," he said. "Live music. Snacks. Drinks. Good people. I swear, it'll be nothing like that other party I dragged you to. What do you say?"

I raised an eyebrow at him, forcing some suspense before giving him a shrug. "Why the hell not?"

Who knew? Maybe it'd relieve my shit-ton of stress.

"Great." He nodded, looking past my shoulders. "Looks like you're up."

"Finally," I breathed, turning around to step up to the desk. I put my student ID onto the surface. "Kathleen Silver. I'm expecting just one package."

"We got you right here," the girl said, hefting a large cardboard box onto the desk and sliding it over to me.

Before I could take it, Elliot stepped around me and up to the desk. I half-expected him to try to flirt with the girl working the mailroom, and I felt my blood pressure rise as he put his hands on my package.

"Are you expecting a package?" the girl asked.

Instead of replying, Elliot pulled my package toward himself, and lifted it into his arms. He turned to me, and said, "Nope. Just here to provide some service to this lovely lady right here."

With that, he tucked the package under his right arm, and began walking away from the mailroom. I watched him, my feet frozen into place as if my mind hadn't registered the fact that I was done with my little errand.

"You just gonna stand there with your mouth open, Silver, or are you gonna thank me?" he called, grinning over his shoulder. "Come on. I'll carry it up for you."

I shook my head down at the ground, a weak attempt to hide the smile slinking across my face. "Thank you. What a gentleman."

Did he really just see me standing in line and decide to join for the sole sake of carrying my shit? If that didn't make me a motherfucking Cinderella, I didn't know what did.

"So," I said, as we waited for the elevator. "Are you going to tell me where this party is, exactly? And, like, who's going?"

"Nope."

I narrowed my eyes at him. Elliot just threw his head back at laughed.

"I'm kidding. I would never withhold such pertinent information from Kathleen Silver. To answer the second part of the question, it'll just be me, myself, and I. Oh, and you, too."

I rolled my eyes. "So, you're asking me out? My bad—*forcing* me out?"

"That would be an accurate statement."

The elevator doors glided open, and a mob of boys spilled out, obviously already too drunk for whatever haunt they were about to infiltrate. We took their place, and I waited for the doors to close behind us before asking him anything more.

"And where will this *date* be taking place?" I said, emphasizing the word *date* as if to test him, to see if he'd flinch or possibly even throw up. After everything that had happened to me over the past few days, that was exactly what *I* wanted to do. "Some park? A Gymnastics studio?"

He chuckled. "God, you're hilarious. No, and no. It's a secret. Can you keep secrets?"

"Maybe," I said. "Tell me and we'll find out."

"Um…" Elliot looked me up and down, as if his eyes were human lie detectors, and he wasn't entirely convinced. "You'll just have to see for yourself. Can I pick you up at your door around… eight? Ish?"

"How about eight on the dot?" I replied.

"Sounds good," he said, just as the elevator doors parted. "Sounds like a real plan."

"You better be there," I said, stepping out of the elevator before him. "Or you'll be in big trouble."

I didn't know why I was doing this. Maybe I was just too lonely and needed a distraction.

"Don't worry," Elliot said as we came to my door. I unlocked it, letting out a sigh of relief to find most of Vivian's things already cleared from our room. "I won't let you down."

10

Once again, I was in my room, combing through my purple hair and slathering my eyelids with matching purple makeup, getting ready for a party that would more likely contribute to the elements of the universe trying to ruin my life instead of keeping it together.

Oh, nostalgia.

Except, this time, I had the room to myself. Instead of reeking of alcohol, or perfume, it smelled of nothing but home. I'd unpacked my box of clothes to find a surprisingly pleasing array of clothing items—dresses I'd forgotten I had, neon fishnet stockings and enough off-shoulder sweaters to make any fall fashionista cringe. AKA, a certain Vivian Russo.

But I didn't have to worry about her anymore, did I?

No. The answer was no. It had to be.

I heard a knock at my door, and before moving toward it, I checked my phone for the time. It was five minutes till eight. Nothing that had happened so far convinced me that it was Elliot who was not only on time, but early. Still, I got hopes up as I walked over to the door. I peered through the peephole and froze as I found myself looking into the bug-eyed versions of Leo and Felix.

Fuck.

"What do you want?" I ground out, trying to sound a little meaner than I should've. "Pussy?"

"Ha-ha. Very funny, Kat," Leo replied, sticking his head closer to the door. "Can we come in?"

"No fucking way, I have a date and I am not going to mess this up tonight." I muttered as I opened the door, putting a hand at my hips as I stood in the doorway, staring at them.

Leo pressed his lips into a solemn grin, stuffing his hands in the pockets of his khakis while Felix just stared at the floor. They looked as if they came to see if I was okay, but neither made a peep.

"Look," I sighed. "If you wanna talk about the meeting, or whatever, make it quick."

Leo blew out a harsh breath, pulled an envelope from his pocket and handed it to me.

I shot him a questioning glance, "What's this?"

"Just open it, Kat."

"It's the least we could do." Felix chirped up while flashing his charming smile.

Once I opened it, I was blown away. It was a round-trip plane ticket to England.

"What's...why... you really didn't have to..." I stuttered. I just couldn't believe it. I mean I know they have enough money to throw around, but to spend it on me... to see Pierre?

"Thank you so much!" I cried as I threw myself towards them.

"You are welcome Kitty Kat. Now," Leo paused, "we also came to talk about you. About... us."

"Us?" I lifted an eyebrow. "There's nothing to talk about."

For a moment, Leo's mischievous smirk flashed across his lips, and stepped forward, closing the space between us, almost completely. The tips of our noses were less than an inch apart, and I could feel his breath, fresh like mint or lemon, against mine. Felix also stepped forward, pushing past me into my dorm room. He situated himself behind me and wrapped his arms around my waist. I didn't struggle... the excitement was getting to me.

Warmth radiated from Leo as he put his hand up against the doorframe, leaning his head in slowly, carefully, toward the crook of my neck.

"You're right," he whispered. "We don't have to talk."

I could feel his hair brushing against my cheek, and as his lips made contact with the skin of my neck, heat flushed through me and down toward my legs.

He was right.

We didn't have to talk.

Without warning, I grabbed Leo by his wrist and tugged him inside, kicking the door shut behind me. Leo pinned me to the back the door, his lips smashing against mine, his tongue digging past my lips as he straddled me against the door. His hands moved up and under my shirt, and I could feel his cool fingertips gliding across my already hot belly and around the small of my back, moving up to my bra.

He bucked his hips against mine, and I let out a small gasp as I felt a bulge growing under the cloth of his pants. Quickly, as he nipped at my collarbone, I snuck my hand behind me to lock the door. As Leo's one hand began undoing my bra strap, his other sunk down to my panties, past the fabric of my skirt. He squeezed my buttocks through the fabric of my panties, pushing me up closer to his growing manhood.

"Leo," I breathed, dipping my head into his neck, and sucking on the flesh. "Just fuck me already."

"Your wish is my command."

He yanked me away from the door, and before I knew it, we were sprawled across my floor, amidst the tossed around changes of dresses and stockings and makeup. Leo bent his head down, lifting my shirt to plant a fat, loud kiss just above my belly button. It caused me to break out in laughter, which only made him continue.

"Oh my God, *stop*," I giggled. "Cut to the good stuff."

"What? This isn't turning you on?" he said, smirking up at me.

"Fuck you," I laughed.

"I will."

"We will," Felix added.

With that, Leo sat back on his knees to undo his pants. Resting my hands under the back of my head, I watched as he unzipped it slowly, and peeled his pants off of his legs and settled back onto top of me. Off to my side, Felix had also freed himself of his clothes and his cock was just as hard as the one pushing down on my pussy. I beckoned Felix too me as I bucked up into Leo. Fuck, I was wet.

Leo pulled off my skirt, and I helped him by kicking off my panties as I tugged my shirt over my shoulders and undid the rest of my bra, tossing it over my head. Leo fell down over me, sucking and licking at my collarbone before lowering his lips to my breasts. Tingles of pleasure shot through me as he nipped and sucked at my flesh, grinding down on me with his hips all at the same time.

Felix pulled me so I laid diagonally on the bed, allowing my mouth access to his manhood as Leo kicked off his boxers. I took the head of Felix's cock between my lips and swirled my tongue around him, eliciting a gasp with each revolution. I smiled around him before taking him further into my mouth. Unfortunately for me, giving Felix a blowjob distracted me from what was happening between my legs. Just as Felix's length was nearing my throat, Leo decided to plunge into me. I gasped and my eyes went wide as I felt him enter me, inch by inch.

This, of course, was hilarious to the two of them, and they both burst out laughing at my reaction. I withdrew Felix from between my lips and passed a harsh look between the pair of naked men.

"Keep laughing and I'll get dressed again, leaving you too hanging."

The boys looked to each other and then back at me.

"Ok, ok," Leo said with a slight grin on his lips. "We get it."

While I had momentarily left Felix high and dry, Leo was still inside of me, and he quickly started picking up his pace. I hummed and moaned as I savored him before remembering I had a second dick to take care of. I reached out for Felix and grabbed his shaft. After a few pumps up and down the length and brought it back to my lips and continued where I had left off.

The three of us quickly fell into a rhythm as my back flexed and gave way to Leo's striding pressure. He was hot inside me and I tightened around him, like he was a part of me. He didn't wait another moment before pulling back and plunging back into me, over and over, harder and harder with each thrust. I could feel him going deeper inside me, as forging a tunnel up into the most sensitive parts of my body, as if he wanted to be the first to do so, as if he were fucking a virgin.

Unlike Elliot, Leo was aggressive, playful with his movements, lifting his chest from mine to smirk down at me as he continued with quick, short little thrusts. When I bucked up against him, he dove back over me, burying his face between my breasts and gave me one deep, hard push, dragging my whole body up the floor a few inches. He owned me, ravished me, and I wanted more.

Then there was Felix. I felt a bit bad as I did my best to give him a sloppy sideways BJ while Leo bounced me around. Though when I looked up and saw the ecstasy on his face, I realized I shouldn't have worried. I focused on his cock, on my lips and tongue, and tried to ignore the heat building between my legs. With my right hand, I reached up grabbed a handful of Felix's ass. I felt his cock twitch in my mouth as I did, and I used the extra leverage to push him forward and back, basically making him fuck my lips. Soon the light gasps turned to groans and I knew he was close.

"Faster Leo," I gasped out as my own undoing approached.

He dipped his face to mine, then nuzzled into my neck as he quickened his pace, his body bouncing on top of me in short, deep strides. I arched my body to keep up with his pace, helping him along as his thrusts reached a certain sensitive point inside me, slamming that certain spongy spot in my body as spurts of euphoria rocked through me.

"Are you close?" he whispered, nipping at my earlobe.

I nodded slightly. "So's Felix," I gurgled out.

Felix nodded. "So close..."

Knowing Felix was only moments away, I moved all my attention to the head of his beautiful cock. I felt it twitch and tense under my assault, and moments, his long groan let me know he was cumming. I kept my lips wrapped around Felix as he came, teasing out each drop of cum until he cried out, "No more! I can't take anymore."

Felix pulled away, his glistening cock still half hard as he flopped down onto the floor. I caught his eye and licked my lips, and I swear his cock get harder as his jaw was slack and eyes still in a post orgasmic blur.

With one man taken care of, I returned my attention to Leo who's slow strokes were maddening. My clit was on fire and my pussy ached... that was all I knew. I could feel my vaginal walls pulse like they were being beat like drums, beat with such intense passion the skin would snap if he continued anymore.

Then, I felt it.

Both of us let out a waterfall of gasps and seething breaths. The familiar twitch I had just felt from Felix between my lips was now happening inside of me. In the heat of the moment, nobody had thought of or brought up condoms. So each pulse of Leo sent a warm sensation deep within me. I relished it and smiled as I came down from my own orgasm while Leo collapsed on top of me. I wrapped my arms around him while his dick still pulsing inside me. His body encased me, and his arms and legs draped over me on either side. The scent of sex filled the room, and in the midst of the puddle of sweat and sighs the three of us created together, I giggled at the thought of Elliot entering the room.

"Okay," I breathed as Leo lifted off of me to lay at my side, his body still practically stuck to mine. "You two should probably go."

"What? You don't want a round two?" Felix asked. "I can be ready in like... 10 minutes?"

I attempted to wriggle away from Leo, and he reluctantly got up to his knees, shuffling away from me. I still laid there on the bed, legs spread wide, pussy pulsing and wet, feeling like the subject of some sensuous postmodern painting. Like a goddess to his humble human being.

Leo was watching me. "We didn't use protection," he said, almost embarrassed.

"I know," I confirmed. "I'm on the pill."

A smile instantly lit up both their faces.

"You're welcome," I said.

"Thank you," Leo replied, standing up over me.

He reached down a hand to help me up, and I took it, squealing as he tugged me up and against him as if I weighed next to nothing. Still naked, my breasts pressing up against his hard chest, I could feel his heartbeat, his breaths slow, and as he leaned into me, I could feel his breath, warm and heavy against my lips, coaxing them open for one last kiss.

We lingered there for a moment, our lips sucking and intertwining within one other, tasting, consuming each other. When I pulled back a hand weaved through my hair and pulled me to the side. My lips then met Felix's and I spent the next few moments going through the same motions with him as I had with Leo. Finally, I pulled back, free of both men's lips before twin hands grabbed my ass, one on each cheek.

"Oh my God, you two are fucking dirty," I laughed, pushing them away. "You both have to go. Now."

Leo's shoulders drooped, and he put on a pout. "But I don't wanna."

"Me neither," Felix added. I pointed down to his semi-erect cock. "See, almost ready for round two."

"Well, you *have* to," I said, snatching Leo's shirt up from the floor to toss it at him. I then found Felix's boxers and held them out on one finger. "Get dressed and go on."

Suddenly, there was a light knock coming from the door. The three of us froze, our eyes strung to the peephole. It could've just been someone walking down the hall from outside, but we couldn't take any chances. Slowly, I tiptoed over to the door and squinted through the peephole.

It was Elliot.

"Just getting dressed," I called out to him. "Be right out!"

Quickly, I turned around to find Leo bending over, convulsing with silent, wheezing laughter.

"Who's that?" he whispered. "Your boyfriend?"

"Shut up," I whispered harshly.

Trying to hide myself behind the door, I opened it slightly and peeked my head out. "Be ready soon." I told Elliot.

Being the 'gentlemen' that he is, Elliot put his hand on the door and began pushing it open. "Oh? Then you won't mind if I come in?" he asked, his tone and eyes both filled with desire.

"I-"

Before I could even start an excuse, Elliot began pushing the door open. I jumped back, doing my best to keep from exposing myself to anyone else in the hallway. Once Elliot had slid inside my room, I pushed the door closed and turned to find his eyes wide as they slowly swept down my naked body.

"Getting dressed?" he asked. "Doesn't look like you've gotten very far." Elliot threw a thumb over his shoulder. "Guessing these two had something to do with it?"

He turned to Leo and Felix. Leo had a sly grin while Felix just shrugged.

"You guys could of at least waited for me," Elliot quipped as he closed the gap between me and him.

He didn't wait for an answer from his friends before his lips claimed mine and his hand cupped my breast. I groaned into his kiss before my lips parted to accept his ravenous want.

"I didn't really want to share," Felix said. "But I guess sharing her with you guys is better than not having her at all."

I heard both Leo and Felix stand and opened my eyes. Both of them were ready for 'round two' as Felix had said only a minute ago.

"Nuh-uh," Elliot chided. "You two had your turn, you're gonna have to wait."

Leo shook his head. "We're here, so we're gonna take part." He turned to me. "As long as you're cool with it, Kat?"

I didn't know what to say. Sure I had fantasized about having Elliot, and occasionally maybe Felix or Leo as well, but never more than one of them at a time and especially not all three. Tongue tied, I just nodded my consent, which caused a smirk to tug at Leo's lips.

"Lady said it's ok," Felix said like it was law. "We're all in."

"Fine," Elliot acquiesced, "But I want her pussy, you two can take turns getting sucked off."

"Deal," Leo and Felix agreed in harmony.

Well, at least I know I have my work cut out for me, I thought.

With the details now worked out, Elliot made quick work of his clothes and joined me and the other two boys in our naked states. His cock was already hard and glistening. Apparently discussing how they were going to take me was enough to turn him on. Elliot stalked over to me a with a deliberate movement he laced one hand into the hair at the back of my head while the other slipped a finger between my legs, landing directly onto my already sensitive clit.

"Oh!" I cried as a bolt of electricity shot from between my legs to my core.

Elliot cut off my cry as he pushed my head forward and crushed his lips into mine. This wasn't just any kiss. He was taking what he wanted from me, claiming me. I let him.

"Bend over," Elliot ordered as he pulled me away. He twisted me around and smacked my ass while I processed what was going on. "I said, bend over." Another crack rang out as he smacked my other cheek.

I didn't waste any more time as I bent over, placing my palms on my bed and present my reddening behind to my former bullies turned lovers.

"Perfect," Elliot said under his breath. "I'm going in," he said louder. "You two do what you want with her mouth."

Leo and Felix didn't hesitate. As I felt Elliot's manhood prod my already slick entrance, I found Felix's cock just to my right and Leo's to my left.

Decisions, decisions.

I turned my head to the left to take Leo's waiting shaft between my lips. I mirrored my movements on Leo's length with Elliot's behind me. With each inch of Elliot penetrating me I took an equivalent amount of Leo into my mouth. Both men groaned as they enjoyed me, and I answered back with a mewl of my own.

"What am I suppose to do?" Felix whined. "Just jerk myself off?"

I released Leo for a moment to say, "I'll get to you, just be patient."

Felix let out a sigh then suggested, "I can take her ass."

"Like hell you will," I answered.

I turned to Felix who had his arms crossed and was continuing to pout. I drug my tongue down his length then back up to the head of his cock before swirling around it then sucking lightly. His pout began to melt away before I pulled away.

"Hey!" he protested.

"I said I'd get to you," I replied.

"Fine."

With Felix satisfied, for now, I returned to Leo while Elliot increased his pace from behind.

"Mmmmm," I purred, then told Elliott "Harder," before I returned to bobbing up and down Leo's dick.

I sucked and fucked in rhythm. I couldn't have done anything else even if I had wanted to. This was all so new that it took all of my concentration just to keep sucking as Elliot pounded me from behind. I was so focused on my task that I wasn't even sure how much time had passed when I heard a sharp intake of breath from Leo.

"Going. To. Cum." He gritted out.

True to his word, I felt Leo's cock begin to pulse and I pulled away, letting his cum splash across my cheek and lips. Once he was empty and his breaths uneven, Leo collapsed down onto the floor next to the remaining three of us.

"Finally!" Felix said and grabbed a handful of my hair. He directed my cum covered lips to his cock and I found I was once again working a cock with vigor as my own orgasm was building thanks to Elliot's rhythmic pumping.

I found myself moaning around Felix and my blowjob technique was surely suffering as my focus was being pulled from Felix to the heat in my core.

"I'm close!" I called to Elliot as I came up from a breath. "Going. To Cum." I echoed Leo's statement from moments ago.

"Do it," Elliot ordered. "Cum for me Kat."

Elliot: My bully, my crush, and now my lover was telling me to cum, and I listened. With a final pump Elliot undid me. The building tension released and all at once I was transported into a quivering, moaning, plane of pleasure. I tried to keep my wits about me, tried to keep pleasuring Felix, but I had no idea if he was enjoying my meager attempts until I felt warm ropes splashing onto my forehead while at the same time Elliot's cock pulsed inside of me, filling me with my second load of cum for the night.

With all three men – and myself – satisfied, I collapsed down onto the bed. Emotions ran through me. From pleasure to exhaustion to... attraction? Or was it... love?

Do I love them? I asked myself. *All three of them?*
***

"We're going to be late to the party," Elliot offered.

"Like that's my fault," I replied.

Having thrown on the clothes I had selected to wear to the party, I glanced in the mirror. Thankfully, my makeup hadn't smeared too much and I was able to quickly get myself back to looking how I wanted.

Once I patted my hair down so it looked a little less scruffy, and scanned the floor for any obvious hints that I'd just gotten down and dirty, I stepped back up to my door, and took in a deep breath before yanking it open. I poked my head into the hallway, checking to make sure nobody would see three men parading out of my room with me. Once I verified the coast was clear I turned to Elliot, Leo, and Felix.

"Shall we?" I asked.

Leo laughed, his voice full, bright, almost too innocent. I might've even believed we were back in our senior year of high school, perhaps in another life, heading out for a genuine first date to a cute restaurant. Instead, the three of us were probably headed to some cruddy party in some jock's basement with the parents out for the weekend. I couldn't get my hopes up too high.

"Whatcha thinkin'?" Felix asked as we approached the elevator. One of the cars had just taken a person, and the doors were about to close before Elliot dashed forward all of a sudden and stuck his hand into the car to keep the doors from closing. We all squeezed in.

"Nothing much," I replied, letting out a breath as I stuck my hand into my purse, tapping the glass of my phone screen. I was so excited to see Pierre and had to let him know I was coming to check on him this weekend after classes had started. After all, we were still best friends. I couldn't help but crack a slight grin, and had to cast my gaze down at the floor so that Felix wouldn't notice and repeat the question. What would I say?

Oh, just thinking about another guy why heading out on a date with three others. You know, nothing much at all.

"You ready for classes to start?" Leo asked as we entered the lobby and headed toward the door.

I glanced up at him and watched as a smile slunk across his lips. It was a silly question, and we both knew the answer. I couldn't believe he was trying to make conversation with me—that any boy besides Pierre would try. They weren't dragging me along to this thing because

I was easy. It wasn't because I had a perfect, round face like Vivian's or a tight enough ass. They genuinely enjoyed my company, or so it seemed.

I wanted to believe it, anyway.

"Of course, I am," I replied sarcastically. "As ready as any college freshman should be."

Elliot chuckled as he held the door open for me. "What are you majoring in, anyway?"

"Don't know," I said, shrugging. We walked along the sidewalk, headed toward the parking lot. "You?"

"I'm thinking about marketing," Leo said proudly, as if it was a field his father had worked in all his life. "Maybe."

"Why marketing?"

"Because," he said, and I could tell he was about to say something stupid that would make me laugh out loud. "I want to be one of those people who make everything seem better than it actually is. Take college, for instance. You've seen the advertisements for this place—has it lived up to your expectations?"

I let out a snort. "That's a hard no."

"See? They did a good job, those salesmen," he said. "They fooled you. Fooled all of us, really. They got us to spend our money."

"So, you want to lie to people," I said, "in order to make money."

"Sure," he replied, like he was lacking a sense of morality.

We headed toward Elliot's car. He took the driver's side, and I settled in the passenger's seat beside him while Leo and Felix climbed in the back. Just as Elliot turned on the engine, I felt my phone vibrate once again, and looked down at it.

Hey, Kat. I'm so sorry for all of this. I hope you can forgive me. You know I will always love you. I am so ready to see you and talk about us. Call me when you can. Love, Pierre

My heart skipped a beat.

I know I can handle three guys now… but could I handle a fourth? More importantly what would Pierre think of the relationship I've found myself in. Would he understand? *Could* he after everything these three men had put us through? I wasn't sure, but I did know that I had to have Pierre in my life.

www.ingramcontent.com/pod-product-compliance
Lightning Source LLC
Chambersburg PA
CBHW061230170626
46809CB00007B/2596